THE MAN ABOVE SUSPICION

JAMES MAYO

The Man Above Suspicion

HEINEMANN : LONDON

William Heinemann Ltd
LONDON MELBOURNE TORONTO
JOHANNESBURG AUCKLAND

First published 1969

© James Mayo, 1969

434 45806 6

Made and printed in Great Britain by
Morrison & Gibb Ltd
London and Edinburgh

HOAX

I

THE CONVAIR overshot the runway at eighty knots. Joanna Dunlop, taut in her seat, saw the lights streaking past the rainy porthole, felt the wheels touch down and roll, roll. . . . Mentally she waited for the braking, the reverse thrust, but they were rolling, rolling, skidding along very fast. Then there was a terrific roar from the reactors, the cabin shuddered and they were abruptly tilting upward as the pilot gunned full power for an emergency climb. Coats slid from the rack above, something crashed in the galley and the toilet doors behind slammed open.

Joanna tried not to move. Her father beside her lifted a forefinger, scratched his moustache. The cabin was filled with a driving electric hum and they began to bump heavily through the cloud.

They levelled out, still bumping. Presently the speaker came on. 'This is the captain speaking. I'm sorry we had to check our touchdown there a moment ago, ladies and gentlemen. The storm conditions reduced our visibility and – uh – inundated the runway. I expect most of you understood what was happening. We're making another approach and I hope we shan't be delayed more than a few minutes. Please keep your seat-belts fastened.' A hostess lurched down the aisle, clinging to the seat-backs, beaming.

Afterwards, in the bus to the terminal, Joanna thought there probably hadn't been much danger. But the nervous mood it had induced wouldn't lift and the rainy Sunday-night streets outside, the dull familiarity of England didn't transmit the usual reassurance. She watched the dim-lit curtains in the back rooms going past. Think of those interiors, the wallpaper and po, the H.P. bedroom suites, the lino, the overpass above you.

Oh, come on, no mood for the evening – dinner with Tim Rayner. She made an effort to throw it off, searched in her bag and lit a cigarette.

'If you're not going to be long, Daddy, we can share a cab.'

'M'm, all right.' His unmoved manner, his Ministry of Agriculture staidness, did not convey a hint of how close they were in fact. She knew he had loved their weekend in Paris, perhaps he even enjoyed the official business, the old conference on Feeding Stuffs or whatever it had been, he never said and she never asked, too boring. They had wandered round the city together today, silently happy; their dependence on each other wasn't vocal. He wanted an early train home to Dorset in the morning because the old Ministry Research Station would collapse without him, they'd lose their experimental tomatoes or something; she'd made up her mind no Art School for her till Tuesday. But *tonight* . . .

She drew on her cigarette, her reflection in the glass riding alongside against the West London roofs and house-fronts, a pale northern face, pale eyelashes and fair hair. She was twenty. At Gloucester Road, the rain had stopped. They took a taxi to the small hotel her father used in the mews at Hyde Park Corner.

'Good evening, Mr Dunlop,' Mrs Dace, alone on Sunday evening duty, greeted them at the reception desk, ex-Kenya and appropriately ostrich-like tonight with her long neck and a new piled-up hair-do. 'Hah was Paris, Joanna? Did you hah fun?' Her neck-sinews lifted her chin like prongs.

'M'm, super. Could I have the key, Mrs Dace? I'm in a terrific hurry.' There was a small red-carpeted hall, cream walls, flowers, stairs up, all brightly lit and snug.

'I've had to move yoh, Mr Dunlop, I'm afraid. It is only for the one night, isn't it?' She turned the register for him to fill in the details. 'You're in 17 and 18.'

'Bath?'

'I'm so sorrah. There's a bathroom and toilet *just* opposite.'

'I'll go on up and change, Daddy. Give me a knock – and be as quick as you can.'

He was downstairs by eight o'clock, fifteen minutes ahead of her, chatting to Mrs Dace between the calls coming through on the small switchboard while he waited. Mrs Dace always claimed they had met during his years in Kenya. The sound of an arriving taxi came from the mews just as Joanna appeared on the stairs. They captured it and he told the driver to leave him at the Hunt Club first.

'You can take him on,' he said to Joanna. 'Have you got any money?'

'Only about ten shillings.'

He gave her a pound. It was Tim somebody, some young man who wanted to be a racing driver. 'Where are you going?'

'I don't know, only to dinner. Soho probably.'

'Well, don't be late.'

'I shan't be. Tim just rang up. He has to go back to Maidstone tonight, something wrong with his car he has to see to first thing in the morning so he's getting the last train.'

The cab ran through the wet streets and they sat wordless in the small isolation watching the lights go by. At the entrance to Marlborough Street, the cab braked in front of a lantern and a yellow Road Up No Entry panel at one side of the road.

'This all right for you, sir? Or you want me to go round?' the driver said over his shoulder. 'This is a new lot, this blockage. Place you want's just up this side, about half-way up.'

'That's all right, this'll do.' Dunlop got out. 'Have a good time, dear.' She was sitting forward on the seat, her face a pale oval just visible in the shadow.

She said, 'I'll come by and pick you up if it's not late.'

'All right. Do.' He smiled and clicked the door shut so that she shouldn't think he wanted to hear where she told the man to go. It was full of these small unspoken things. He heard the cab make a U-turn behind him.

*

The rain began to fall heavily again at 10.30 and continued without a break for another hour. At 11.40 when a cab turned into Marlborough Street and pulled up at the door of the club, it was beginning to slacken. Joanna said, 'Please wait,' adjusted the scarf over her head and dashed across. At the top of the steps the porter pulled open the door. 'Good evening, Miss.'

'Mr Dunlop, please. I'm his daughter. Lord, what weather!'

The porter, a short man with a quiff, looked at her with his mouth open and Joanna had the impression that she was expected. 'Would you wait, Miss?'

She knew it was best to go no farther than the vestibule of this male territory and stood looking in across the marble-floored entrance with its busts, candelabra, bird's-eye maple panels, varnished portraits and black leather-topped seats; a staircase curved elegantly up beyond.

Her mind was full of the unexpected gentleness of the evening, of Tim's good looks and strength, this new hope he had of getting a Formula chance – he was changing fast, deepening, she had lost her dominant role in their relationship and liked it better. She stood thinking about him, turned, looking out into the wet black street.

Presently she realized that she had been waiting rather a long time. Where was the porter? Nobody was moving inside the club and she couldn't hear anything. It couldn't be far from midnight and on Sunday there surely weren't many members still about.

Then a tall bald middle-aged man with a grey army moustache was coming towards her followed by the porter.

'Good evening, Miss Dunlop? I'm Colonel Chambers, the Secretary. You were looking for your father?'

'Yes. How do you do?' Mentally she bet his nickname was Jerry.

'We've only got his Dorset address here. It's Greengates House, Buck—'

'Oh, no!' she laughed. 'He's in the club, he's here now. I told him I'd call for him.'

A small pause.

'Mr Dunlop has not been here tonight.'

'What?'

He was leaning down to her and she looked up into his large globular grey eyes, catching the pungency from the red snuff handkerchief hanging out of his breast pocket, his general tobacco, booze and something smell. The colonel's face was a little strange; she could see the tip of his tongue, between moustache and lower lip, moving up and down. It made a faint tick . . . tick . . . tick, while he stood there bent, his eyes steadily on her.

'But I dropped him here myself, tonight. About eight o'clock.'

'He has not been here.'

She jerked her chin back, blinking at him uncomprehendingly, feeling the beginning of fear moving up and hearing now in the sudden intense stillness – the rain had stopped – the other quicker, urgent click-click-click-click of the taximeter at the kerb below. 'But I tell you – I left him.'

'No.'

'Are you sure? He must be—'

'Quite sure.'

Her eyes shifted and she saw that another porter had come out from somewhere inside and a fourth man, younger, in dark clothes. The four were standing quite still, watching her. The colonel's bald head, spotted by small brownish marks, swam before her like ectoplasm and it was the strange silent observation of them all, the hint of something parallel to reality that caught hold of her and destroyed her attempt to treat it as a simple mis-understanding, a mistake. *Something else was happening*.

'Please . . . ask the staff.'

Colonel Chambers's blob-head shook and suddenly she had the same panic she had had in the aircraft, wanting to escape quickly, run . . . these men watching her . . . she spun on her heel, wrenched open the outer door and clattered down the steps to the cab.

'Quickly, Hallet Place Hotel.'

She slammed the door, sat pressed back tensely on the seat. What should she do? She fumbled out a cigarette and lit it. Who were those men? Was it true he'd not been there? After all, she hadn't seen him go into the club. Perhaps he had changed his mind at the last minute. She hadn't *seen* him. Look, don't be so stupid, stop drama-tizing the thing, he's probably walking back . . . not in this weather . . . well, with a friend or something, it's utterly mad behaving like this, don't be a little idiot.

Gradually she forced herself to calm down.

The rain came on again as the cab reached Hallet Place. She sat inside, bent over her bag, finding change, paid and got out. The light from the hotel entrance shone through the glass doors on to the wet pavement. She pulled one door open, walked in brushing the rain off and looked up. The shock made her check – the man behind the counter wasn't the right one.

He was a stocky man with white hair and a broad face, standing quietly watching her as if he were waiting for her. Then she realized that he must be the night porter who had come on duty since she and her father had left the hotel – and in one moment the whole situation slipped back into normal, the commonplace. She went forward, the man smiled; she saw he was wearing a porter's striped coat.

'Good evening, Miss,' he said pleasantly.

'Good evening. Seventeen please. Is my father in? Mr Dunlop? Room 18?'

The porter turned to the keyboard behind him, unhooked a key and handed it over. 'Yes, Miss, he's in.'

Relief flooded through her, she smiled and said 'Thank you. Goodnight', then swung back. 'Oh – a call in the morning. Half past seven, please.'

'Certainly, Miss. Tea?'

'No, thank you.' She went upstairs, thinking she had been ridiculous, melodramatic. Potty, the whole thing; must have been the plane. She turned at the top of the first flight, crossed the landing and went up to second, turning right along the corridor towards the quieter back of the hotel. Red carpet and cream walls; everything quiet, nobody about, not a voice or a radio from behind the doors; the hotel had no licence and only a breakfast room below. At the door of room 18, she said, 'Daddy – you awake?'

'H'm?'

'Can I come in?'

'Allow me, Miss.' She jumped a little – it was the porter who had come soundlessly upstairs behind her, reaching past her, fitting his pass-key into the Yale lock.

'Thank you.'

The door swung open under his push and she took a step inside. There was only one small light on on the far side of the room by the washbasin where he was standing with his back to her. She stopped and he turned round, a man with a long fleshy face.

She felt a great plunge of terror. 'That is not my father.'

The man smiled and said to the porter, 'My daughter is not quite herself sometimes. Would you mind, nurse?'

Joanna's back bumped the porter behind her as a woman stepped out from behind the door and took her arm. The porter said, 'It's all right, Miss,' before the woman's hand stopped her scream.

*

[7

*

Page one, column six top *Daily Express*:

'VOODOO MAN' IN
PARK MYSTERY

The man found in a state of distress in St James's Park
early yesterday morning was identified last night as Mr
Bernard Dunlop, 51, of Buckminster, Dorset, a former
resident of Kenya, who said he was a 'government research
chemist'. St George's Hospital staff said last night that
Mr Dunlop appeared to have been attacked but was
not able to give a coherent account of what happened.
When found, his clothes were torn, he had cuts on face
and hands and broke away from passers-by who tried
to help. An ambulance was called and after some
difficulty he was caught and taken to St George's.

Mr John Wallis, a bus conductor of Randall's Lane,
E.6, who helped control Mr Dunlop said, 'He was
running about like mad, gibbering sort of. Made me
think of a man who got the voodoo in him, like I have
seen plenty times in my home in Jamaica. He was that
shaking and he was running away wild and he couldn't
hardly talk he was so dead scared.'

Stop Press below on the same page:

'VOODOO MAN' (see Page 1)

Home Office said unknown persons staged hoax early
yesterday in St James's Park, one claiming to be senior
civil servant just back from official visit to France.
Three men were taken to Vine Street but later released.
Home Office said students appeared to have put on
hoax as elaborate and obscure joke.

Reporters at the Home Office and St George's later in
the day were given a few extra details. They led nowhere.

OPEN END

2

'THEY TELL me tiger semen's in great demand – you must be making a killing,' Charles Hood said and Belgeorge's eye gave an amused glint.

'No – but look at those. Aren't they beautiful? Purple coots from Ceylon.' He pointed to the group of long-legged birds with deep purple plumage and bright red bills stepping delicately across the slope.

'What are those?'

'Sacred ibis. Over there's a demoiselle crane. Pretty?'

In the bright morning light, everything was clear-cut – the trees green, a puddle here and there on the path and the Gloucestershire sky swept free of the weekend rain. Belgeorge's idea of a walk round his private zoo straight after breakfast hadn't sounded much fun to Hood but to his surprise it was turning out to be a great pleasure – landscaped green spaces, streams, good-looking arrangements of rock, a lot of costly trees and shrubs, natural arenas and everywhere free-ranging animals, not a cage or a barrier visible. It was a rich man's indulgence.

'I like to think it's like some vision of eventual paradise, men and animals in perfect communion,' Belgeorge said, the sort of slightly inflated thing you expected him to say, yet who could doubt his sincerity?

Glancing at him now, Hood thought it was the perfect head for Sir Harry Belgeorge, M.P., J.P., philanthropist and moralist, a Hotspur in great causes – forehead, nose and chin cut in stone, finely made lips, a spirited eye. His hair, beginning to grey at the sides, fell thick and handsome, enhancing the nobility; it was certainly the face for women – the face for an actor and of course Belgeorge

[9

was a bit of an actor. The reference books said he was forty – which would have been amazing for what he had done; he was ageless.

They turned down a new path, Belgeorge put a small soundless whistle to his mouth and the empty slope became alive with monkeys.

'Fun,' Hood said.

'They're little black apes from the Celebes,' Belgeorge said, '*Cynopithecus niger*. Very nice fellows.' The monkeys were tail-less with little tufts of hair on their heads and old men's faces and they all seemed to recognize Belgeorge, two pulling gently at his trousers for food.

'Don't they escape?' Hood said.

'No, no. They feed here very happily, so they don't want to go. They're like the barbary apes of Gibraltar – related to them in fact.' He distributed a few peanuts. 'You see, the social order's quite clearly defined. These ones here, the dominant males, have the supreme rank, they're the leaders, the *élite*, though it's a word I don't like. The others stay back, those there, they're the outer ring and they don't interfere, they know it's not their business – they have their own classes, their leaders and inferiors. It is the natural order.'

Hood nodded, repressing a grin; nothing like a zoo for a little unobtrusive morality. But he liked Belgeorge, a man of character – compared with some of the rich men he knew in the contemporary jungle, he was an eighteenth-century humanist.

They strolled on past grazing zebra, a pair of giraffes sailing by beyond. 'I'm setting up an insectarium,' Belgeorge was saying. 'Costly things, insects. Eat vast quantities of fodder, whole lorry-loads – but their organization is fascinating. Excuse me – do carry on.' He bent to shake a stone out of his shoe and Hood, three paces ahead, rounded a clump of shrubs and froze. A black-maned lion, a few feet away, was looking straight at him, head lifted. There was nothing between them, not a bush or a twig on the open ground.

Hood stood rooted, hardly breathing, the lion gave a throaty rumble, slowly lowered his head and shoulders, looking fixedly at Hood and gathering himself. Hood realized he was about to spring.

'Christ—' Reports of zoo accidents, animals loose, boys trapped, rushed through his mind – no longer idiotic. He took a step back, swung round and saw Belgeorge looking on – and understood. It was some favourite gag. He turned back, walked gingerly a pace or two towards the lion, his eyes going over the open ground ahead – then saw the moat. The lion was on the far side. It was an optical illusion, very cleverly done. 'Whew!' He sagged; Belgeorge came up chuckling.

'I thought that was the last stop,' Hood said. 'Even now that trench looks pretty damn narrow to me. Are you sure he can't jump it?'

'He can't. Every animal has a maximum leap and that's just a bit too wide for him. Besides, if you look, you'll see that dip behind and the rocks; there – see? They're to stop him getting the momentum for a jump.'

'I'll be damned.'

'A tiger needs a bit more; and with a tiger you couldn't have a moat with water because tigers like to swim.' They stood admiring the lion who had been joined by a lioness and another male, then Belgeorge said, 'Come here, I want to show you a real rarity.'

He headed down a path under trees. As they breasted the rise, a manservant from the house came round the corner sweating and looking as if he had been searching the park for them.

'Telephone, sir,' he said to Belgeorge.

'What? Tell them to put it through to the pavilion here.'

'It's continental, sir, I think.'

'Oh – Oh well then, yes.' Belgeorge turned to Hood. 'Do excuse me, my dear Hood. It's something I must attend to.'

'Of course.' Hood was about to say he had to go himself but Belgeorge was already walking away with the man, bending his head and quietly speaking to him. Hood lit a cigarette and walked slowly along under the gigantic Syrian plane trees in the general direction of the house.

The weekend at Belgeorge's had been fun and beautifully managed – Belgeorge knew everybody, there had been fifteen people at dinner last night, a mixture of politicians, actors, doctors, painters, two Nobel prize winners and, among the others, a lovely negro girl, a singer named Cal Taylor, whom Hood had got to a piano afterwards and made her sing softly for him. She had sung 'I Should Care' and the old Maxine Sullivan swing version of 'Loch Lomond' and she knew the favourite number of Hood's late great friend Rubirosa, 'I Never Slept a Wink Last Night' – and sent him with it! He hadn't seen her this morning and wondered if she'd already gone.

He looked at his watch – five to nine. Sir James Lovatt, Chairman of Banner Oil, one of The Circle, the consortium of great City firms for whom Hood worked as confidential agent, had rung up last night and wanted to see him in London this morning. It had sounded urgent. He finished the cigarette and stepped out towards the house. On the terrace, the butler said, 'What time would you like the car, sir?'

'Can I have it in about ten minutes, Tanner?'

'Yes, sir. You've been packed, sir.'

'Good.'

By the time Hood had written a note with his phone number and left it for Cal Taylor, the chauffeur had the silver-blue Bentley at the front steps of the house. Arthur Young, Belgeorge's secretary, came out. 'Sir Harry's still on the phone, Mr Hood, and says will you excuse him. He expects you firmly tonight at Belgrave Square, the reception.'

'Yes. Please tell him I'll try to get there.' Hood gave him a smile and shook hands, got in and the car purred down the drive.

*

A two-line advertisement in the Personal column of *The Times* was ringed in red:

Sigma ETA Wednesday Contact without
delay. – Box 1714 T, The Times

Hood lifted an inquiring look at Sir James Lovatt, laid the paper on the desk and dropped into the deep armchair opposite.

'We thought it might be a clue to the man we're after,' Lovatt said, 'but it turns out to be a mind-control therapy clinic.' He held out a Cartier cigarette box and Hood heaved himself forward and took one.

Lovatt's office at the top of the Banner building was a handsome room with a golden-bronze carpet, an illuminated map of the Banner oilfields round the world and a Mossu Desiderio which Hood had found the year before in a secondhand dealer's in Udine and bought for very little. They lit their cigarettes and Lovatt sat back, hooking his arm over the back of the chair, a neat, small-made man with fair hair and moustache. He had been Olympic sabre champion and Hood somehow always thought of this when they met and he looked at Lovatt's compact figure and his light grey eyes.

'What's your flying licence, Charles?'

'An A.'

'Could you fly an air survey?'

'What, for oil? I dare say – if the aircraft isn't too sophisticated. I don't know anything about survey gear though.'

'That's no difficulty. Simple procedure.'

[13

Hood knew he had to listen very carefully and he watched Lovatt's face. Lovatt swivelled in the chair, lifted an ankle to his knee. 'Well, here's the thing. We're interested in a small island in the Caribbean, St Kilda's. You know the story?'

'Bits of it, I think.'

'It used to be British, one of the Windward group, but broke away and went for independence. There was a row, a charade in New York and in the U.N. but the Windwards didn't really care much since St Kilda's was only artificially part of their group anyway – it's a good deal nearer the Venezuelan coast than the rest of them – and they couldn't see they were losing much more than prestige, so they finally let it go.

'The breakaway, as it turned out, was unlucky. The man who brought it off, the one big local figure, a very fine man called Olympio Messenger, got killed accidentally while he was in Washington trying to raise American aid and the result was the island rapidly sank into poverty. It hadn't been rich at the best of times since sugar collapsed in the 1840s and it wasn't strategically valuable. The Americans weren't interested in a few more oranges, nutmegs and bananas and Whitehall cared less.

'About eighteen months ago, we became interested in the offshore oil prospects. We made an approach and got a brush-off. We found that somebody had got hold of the island. We don't know who they are but ever since they've been there, the islanders have kept everybody else off. The only people who have got a toe in are the World Health Office who sent a party down there because there were reports of some outbreak; they were politely corralled for forty-eight hours and then packed off. We've even been told that a small plane has been shot down in the area, we can't confirm it but if it's true it could mean that somebody has been trying to pirate an offshore oil survey – you can take a good survey over water nowadays from the

14]

air, give you enough data to decide whether test drilling's worth while. These things tend to confirm our view that the place is worth looking at.'

Hood nodded.

'We know that just over a year ago, the Venezuelan oil boys were snooping around the island. At some time or other since then they dropped out. Why, we don't know; and they're a tough lot who aren't easily choked off. It's a mystery how the place is surviving economically. There have been rumours that one of the American independents is in there.'

'For oil?'

Lovatt nodded. 'But there's nothing you can get a firm line on. What we want to do is to get somebody in there, to the island, and find out who the people are and what they're doing. And how we can get in. The difficulty has been to discover how to do it.'

'Tourist visa?'

Lovatt said, 'They don't issue any. However, we have found out that somebody to do with the island has offered a job to a pilot named Ed Conroy. Conroy's a crook, though he wasn't always one. He used to work for one of our companies and we still want him for taking off with £8,000 of the firm's money. We've been tipped off by an ex-girl-friend of his in the firm – who doesn't want to see him because she's scared of him – that he is coming to London this week.

'Conroy hasn't told her who the people are. She thinks he's after more money before he goes in with them. He is obviously going to keep his head down while he's here. He is *not* supposed to make contact with them, simply signal his presence – possibly by a code ad in the paper – and they will communicate. We thought this might be the ad but it isn't.'

'Can't you get the girl to play along and—?'

'We have. She's agreed to see Conroy when he turns

up and tip us off. At a suitable moment we will get the police to pick him up and you step into his place.'

'Suppose he has buck teeth and faultless Lithuanian?'

'Well, he hasn't. He's your build, you could pass. Anyway, as far as we know these people haven't seen him yet.'

Hood drew on the cigarette, watching Lovatt's face. 'But when the police arrest him, it'll be reported and they'll see it, won't they?'

'It's a chance we have to take. We've got a charge out against him in Aberdeen and he'll be taken up there. There's at least a good likelihood it won't be noticed. The French want him too and he skipped bail once before so they won't let him loose.'

'H'm.'

'If it makes you feel any better, he's been in for assault. He's no daisy and the people he is mixed up with aren't either.'

'How are you going to know where he is when he gets here?'

'Well, that's it. We shan't,' Lovatt said. 'We're having to rely on the girl. She has a small flat in town but he may be too chary to go there. But one way or another we shall get to him through her.'

'I see.' There it was in all its simplicity, Hood thought, the sort of assignment with absolutely none of the blanks filled in, an open-ender. Across the desk, Lovatt's eyes held him with a trace of needling – cutlass-tip raised. *Come on, lost your nerve?*

'All right,' Hood said.

'Good.'

A phone on the desk buzzed but Lovatt took no notice. 'Let's talk again later today. See Bill Brady and get two things. First you want Conroy's life story; we have all the dope on him. Second, get Brady to talk to you about the sort of oil equipment to look for on St Kilda's, if you get there. You have to know how to operate a seismograph and the air survey gear. We could meet at . . . five-thirty – no, wait . . . at six I'm at Belgeorge's. Let's—'

'So am I, we can go together.'

'Yes – at Belgeorge's? All right, then.'

They stood up and moved across the room, then Lovatt stopped and put a friendly hand on Hood's shoulder. 'Charles, I don't want to mislead you on this and I don't want you to misunderstand it. We can't tell what's in the situation but we believe, if you get in, it may be . . . very unpleasant.'

Hood looked at him.

'Atlas Oil sent a man to have a look,' Lovatt said. 'You remember T. T. Lucas?'

Hood nodded, picturing the big pleasant man, an ex-Harlequins full-back.

'We don't know how far he was along the line but his wife got a parcel. It had a right hand in it and eight toes, shot off. Posted in Miami.'

'Christ!'

'Lucas never reappeared. They obviously killed him.'

They stood there for a few seconds more looking at each other; Hood saw that Lovatt was uncomfortable and knew he was asking a lot, then Hood nodded. 'Five-thirty.'

'Thanks, Charles.'

In the outer office, Jackie Added, Lovatt's chief secretary, took up a pile of papers to go in. She threw Hood a look as if she knew about the assignment and Hood felt he had to carry it off somehow. He said, 'Added any lately?'

'One thing, you've not been too long for once.' She turned.

'Well, all the days are not equal.' Hood gave her backside a pat. 'And I have my long days, sweetheart, as you know.'

[17

SLEEPING PARTNER

3

THERE WERE police outside the house on the north side of Belgrave Square, passers-by had stopped to watch arrivals, and the crowd filling the main room downstairs overflowed through the french windows into the garden behind.

It was a *coup d'oeil*, Hood thought, looking it over from the stairs – a royal duke, Prince Bernhard, most of the art world, Ministers, the Opposition, coveys of foreign ambassadors and attachés, the C.I.G.S. and the service chiefs, a large number of British and American tycoons – some of whom Hood had never seen in public before – top men in medicine, besides the Foreign Office and civil service, the law and the City. Plenty of pretty women too.

Who else in London at this moment could have pulled in all these people but Belgeorge? It was remarkable. He noticed another Lord Bishop – there must be at least five – talking to a model. Across on the left, under a Duccio crucifixion, Belgeorge had a group round him and guests were pressing up to shake hands.

Hood plunged into the swim. This was, of course, all in aid of The Movement, Belgeorge's enterprise for promoting international amity – and a faint earnestness, a whiff of solemnity and moral uplift hung over even so brilliant and diversified a gathering. Hood grinned; this was the atmosphere Belgeorge seemed to engender, a sort of higher gravity and of course goodness. An immensely good man, Belgeorge, a man of the highest motives. (Nehru had been an admirer.) Yet it didn't entirely explain the success of The Movement. Belgeorge's personal magnetism did something, his good looks and the nobility of his character more still. But there must be something else again.

The Movement was very rich, nearly as rich, they said, as the Ford Foundation. It collected names. Belgeorge personally knew heads of state, the leading men all over, invited them, stayed with them. He did a very skilful publicity job for himself, Hood thought, and was a past-master at putting The Movement over and getting money for it.

Across the room, the Marchioness of Kyle, a noted skinflint, was cooing at Belgeorge with her purple lips. Belgeorge had them all hypnotized. The Movement, Hood had just heard, had got itself given another great house in Washington by the Alvins, no less, the hermit-like American family who were so rich that the Fortune listings never reached into their category.

Hood steered in among the backs and shoulders, greeting here and there. He negotiated a violet backside, ducked past an archimandrite's beard, was checked by a waiter with a great silver tray of drinks and took one.

Six months back, The Circle had told Hood that in view of the big men mixed up with The Movement, it wanted some intelligence on it. Could there be anything that in crude terms you would call pressure, manipulation? Were its political assumptions what they appeared to be? Belgeorge knew all these politicians. The Movement always *seemed* – The Circle had said – to be trying to use political influence at a rather puerile level with a good deal of earnest exhortation and had a host of eminent people at least paying lip-service to it if nothing more.

Was it just high-falutin' moral talk? Was it We-ism and They-ism? What was the involvement? Hood, they said, could get closer in than many others since he already knew people who were associated with it. So Hood had begun cultivating Belgeorge and this had led to weekend invitations – the latest, one of several – and his being here tonight.

A Turkish moustache near by was saying, '. . . world

problems . . .' A Scottish ecclesiastic said, '. . . wurruld conscience . . .'

Hood weaved past, trying to keep out of reach of the Dowager Lady Uke beyond, and ran gently into silk. She turned, a stunning girl holding a champagne glass, and looked at Hood with deep blue eyes.

'Denver, last May,' Hood said. 'We slept together.'

She shook her head.

'It was on the flight to New York. You were across the aisle, I've never forgotten.'

She smiled.

'I recognize your nose. When you dream it wrinkles.'

She laughed. She was tanned a light amber, a high-boned face with a little beauty-spot merging into the right eyebrow – an extraordinarily touching and attractive effect – and honey-coloured hair cut short. The outline of her lips was perfect and she looked fresh and amusing in her short two-tone brown silk frock with a leaf design and a single pin in front.

'You can't find a haircut as short as that nowadays in the Brigade of Guards,' Hood said. 'I think it's adorable.'

'Who are you?' She was smiling.

'Charles Hood. I design refrigerators. What's your name?'

'Kim McCaine. I bet you're weak on the deep freeze.'

Hood laughed. 'Alone?'

'I came with J. D. Morell, but I seem to have lost him.'

J. D. Morell . . . Fibre-glass, was it? Or packaging? No great captain, at all events, as Hood remembered it. A ballet enthusiast or opera amateur, he seemed to recall.

'I hardly know anybody here,' she said. 'Who's that, talking to the girl in green?'

Hood looked over – a thin, chinny old man like one of Feliks Topolski's shaky ancients. 'That's Sir Magnus Opum. Every time the Prime Minister brings him into a speech he calls him Sir Magnum Opus. You can see he's just telling that girl, "Thank you, my dear. I'd prefer a little white torso".'

They laughed. She seemed a little shy, which he liked. She said, 'How do you know these people, Harry Belgeorge and so on?'

'I just wandered in. You need another drink.' He led her through the crush to the nearest table, hoping Morell – whom he had never seen – wouldn't appear and break it up. When they had glasses he said, 'What do you do?'

'Oh, vaguely, I'm in cosmetics.'

'What, "Shed the years with essence of royal grasshopper duct"?'

'Yes. And moontears.'

He snapped a light to her cigarette. 'Let's have dinner and go on for some free association somewhere?' She looked at him with a smile and for a moment he thought she was going to say yes, then she shook her head. 'I can't. I have a plane to catch.'

'We'll share the plastic asparagus. Tell me where you're going?' She drew on her cigarette, her eyes on him and said, 'Well, I ought—' Abruptly they both stepped back as the crowd near them surged and broke and a tall, gaunt, hawklike woman in a hat stalked out. She was carrying a poodle.

'Yeah, yuh, yuh – just here. Great.' A skinny photographer with crinkly straw hair behind her was flapping an arm. 'Uh, Lady Firebrace, I'm surry it hasta be this way. Y'know a picture of Klaus von Hemmelstock's really worth more *time* and – I was trying to explain on the phone I flew in from N'York specially two weeks ago, ma'am—'

'Get on with it!'

'Yuh . . . I sure appreciate this is the only opportunity. We're hoping this is going in with the Duchess of Windsor's pugs, ma'am.'

A young man in Himalayan pink was bent over the dog combing and fiddling with it. Hood looked round to catch the girl's eye – but she wasn't there. He edged out, searched round and then saw her moving out towards the door on the other side with a man. J. D. Morell, no doubt. He felt a stab – she was lovely.

'Damn,' he said.

CONTACT

4

HOOD HEARD the phone over the roll of the sliding seat and the creak of the tension discs. He stopped pulling on the oars of the sculling machine and stood up, breathing hard. Reaching for a towel, he wiped the sweat off. The gym where he worked out adjoined his flat at the top of the Jordan Mathews Building and was a luxury he never ceased to enjoy. Before the rowing he had skipped rope till it hurt.

He wound the towel round his neck, pulled on a robe and went for the door. The clock said six-thirty. The sound of the evening traffic was faint this far up.

The morning before – something under thirty-six hours since Hood's meeting with Lovatt – Conroy's girl, who was named Gwen Mason, had reported Conroy's arrival. Conroy had moved fast, taken a service flat using the name of Edward Wake and it had promptly become evident that he was set for a quick in and out. Moreover, he obviously had some method of communication with the other party already laid on.

Inside an hour, Conroy had made two phone calls from the flat, then later, about eleven at night, had gone out and taken a call, apparently timed, at a public call-box. Gwen had followed him to the box unseen, leaving the flat door on the latch but had been too scared to get close. This morning she had reported that she believed Conroy had come to some agreement with the other party, who-ever they were.

Outside in the gym entrance, Hood picked up the phone. 'Hello.'

It was Brady. 'This is it. Gwen's just phoned us. He's pulling out in twenty-four hours, he's only waiting for one thing more so she's sure now the deal's fixed. He took another call at a public box just after lunch. Doesn't want to show himself too much – understandable – but she's got something arranged and says she can get him outside in about fifteen minutes. We're getting the police to pick him up quietly as soon as the two of them are away from the building. Gwen has lifted the spare key to the flat and she's leaving it under the central heating radiator in the hall. Get it?'

'Yes.'

'So will you move in right away?'

'I hope that girl's going to get a fat rise.'

'It's laid on.'

'What's Conroy wearing?'

'Dark brown suit, bronze leather shoes, check shirt, greenish tie. No hat. Don't forget he's calling himself Edward Wake. You've got the passport?'

'Yes.' The Banner resources had supplied him with a bogus Canadian passport in the name of Edward Wake – which, of course, Hood would not use – and a good fake Belgian *carte de résident* in the name of Conroy.

'She says he's suspicious, so watch it,' Brady said. 'And you may have visitors.'

'All right.'

'Got the address?'

'Yes.'

'Good luck, old boy. Send us a postcard.'

'You bet.' Hood put the phone down, walked through to the bathroom and took a quick shower. He dried off, went into the bedroom and picked a suit and shirt. The Mason girl certainly had pluck. Conroy didn't sound much fun and she had had to play it along as if she were enjoying things. Hood hoped nothing went wrong for her at the last minute. Conroy's friends had moved fast! But of course there were a hundred ways to pass an address on to somebody if you had it lined up – a phone call to a tourist office or a bookie, a shop to ask for a catalogue.

Hood checked over his money, loaded the Colt Cobra .38 and stuck it into his belt holster. His packed bag had been left at the flat in advance with the porter.

It was a mild evening, a tiger sky. At the Bank, he caught a taxi and told the driver to go to the corner of Devonshire Street. He stopped it a few yards short, paid the man and walked round to the entrance of the block. A woman in a parked car was digging into her handbag. Hood got a good look at her but couldn't see anybody else who might be keeping watch.

The entrance and stairs of the building were a touch flashy – pastel pink carpet, mirror-topped console, glass chandelier, the paint thumbed, mirrored fingerplates on the doors, a lingering scent. He fished out the key from under the radiator, went up to third and opened the door of 3A.

For a second or two he checked, catching the drift of cigarette smoke. Were they still there? Then he went forward. The biggish living-room was empty, so was the bedroom – bed unmade, open suitcase spilling clothes – dressing-room and bathroom. The style was neo-cinema crossed with *haute couture* – crocus-blue carpet, mirror-topped tables, crinkly pink lampshades with bows, two prints of long-necked Louis-Gabriel Domergue girls in gold-dusted frames. The lid of the lavatory seat had a quilted chintz cover. A smart tart's flat? The decor depressed him. Well, anyway, here he was.

He lit a cigarette, wandered back to the living-room. Next move was theirs. If Conroy had been set to leave in twenty-four hours they were probably going to produce whatever he had been waiting for soon. Hood wished he knew just a little of what to expect.

He collected some ice from the kitchen, crossed to the drinks trolley and made himself a vodka martini. The glasses were baccarat and the vodka was Stolovaya, straight from Moscow. There was a hi-fi by the big settee and he turned the switch, watched the arm twiggle on. Ray Charles, 'Ah gotta woman'. Well, well, how about that now? He took a swallow of drink, thinking of Kim McCaine's fresh mouth and lusting for her.

Aaah gotta wooooo-ooo-maan . . .

He carried the drink into the bedroom, put it down and went carefully through Conroy's jumbled suitcase – clothes, a flashlight, street-map of Beirut, two boxes of Hepatogene tablets and a paperback *The Complete Pubic Hair Collector*. He did everything piece by piece and there wasn't a clue. The drawers in the room, the trousers and sports jacket hanging up held nothing.

Hood finished the drink and stubbed his cigarette. It was uncomfortably warm and he slung his coat on a chair, dropped his gun and holster in the suitcase. He took his time and searched the entire flat and at the end had come up with three bills and a mildewed Post Office Savings Book – 8/6d undrawn – in the name of Miss Zoe Gardner, from the kitchen.

It was dark now. He had all the lights on, the flat brightly lit and the curtains undrawn. The place was remarkably quiet, not a sound outside or in. As he went back into the main room, the phone rang. Before he could reach it, the ring cut off. He stood still. It rang again. He lifted the hand-set. 'Yes? . . . Hello? . . .' speaking in a crisp neutral tone.

The line was open but nobody answered. 'Hello?' Nobody. He put the phone back, listening for the corresponding tink of somebody ringing off at the other end but it didn't come. A code call? A signal to summon Conroy to the call-box for further orders?

He found some magazines and sat down. An hour went by. The place was silent and there were no more phone calls. From time to time, Hood got up and moved about so that anybody watching from outside might see that he was there. As the clock struck ten, he caught a light in a window opposite – a girl undressing. She was down to bra and pants, sitting on a chair peeling her second stocking – a crop-head blonde with a lovely figure. She threw the stocking somewhere to the right beyond Hood's range of vision, reached back, unhooked the bra, shrugged and let it drop. Hood let out an admiring 'Whew!' – it would have raised a whistle at any strip show – shell-pink nipples pouting on perfect breasts, bigger than they had looked in the bra and joggling gently like moulded blancmange.

She ducked out of the pants, threw them right too with the bra and stood up showing a flat belly and a blonde thicket at the V-site.

Hood thought she was sweet.

She was speaking to somebody 'off' on the right where she had thrown the clothes. Next moment she had turned, reached for a phone and stood talking. First she turned sideways, one arm folded under her breasts, lifting and pointing them, then swivelling and raking him with twin nipple-fire da-da-da-da, crooking a knee and laughing into the phone. Slowly her free arm dropped, smoothing her belly, fingers gently caressing the golden road to Samarkand until he thought she was . . . well *wasn't* she . . . ? Then she stretched, rang off and disappeared. He watched a moment longer – and the light went out. Lucky devil, Hood thought, whoever he was.

He poured himself another drink, went into the bedroom, then stood listening. There had been a small sound from the other room. He put the glass down, facing the door, and in a moment heard a faint metallic chink-chink approaching.

Slowly the door swung full open and a girl came in, a cool, leggy blonde in a dark blue dress with a metal belt. She didn't even jolt when she saw him, stopped just inside the doorway looking Hood up and down, flicked a glance over the rest of the room, then back at Hood.

'How do you do?' Hood said.

[27

'Good evening.' She looked him over again with cool self-possession.

'Just passing?' He was on the point of asking her how she had got in then caught himself. Conroy or the other party might have left her a key. She took a step farther into the room, her chain belt chinking.

'How did you guess?' she said.

'I took night-school courses.'

Her thick hair was pulled round to the back of her neck – he thought of Courbet's pictures of girls' hair – and the clear line of her jaw, with the little hollow under her cheekbone, made her look cool and chic.

'No char?' Her look indicated the unmade bed.

'She's unreliable.'

'How much is it, do you know?'

'Well, they used to charge thirty shillings a lash, twenty guineas for a black mass—'

'The rent.' She wasn't amused.

Was this a code-exchange to which he was supposed to supply the answers? He gave her a smile, 'Sorry, you must be from the Customs and Excise?'

She came farther into the room, looking it over then turned back towards the main room. 'A friend told me there was a flat to let. I saw the door on the latch and supposed it was empty, so I came in to see.'

He hadn't left the door on the latch; they'd given her a key. 'Anybody I know, your friend?' he said pleasantly.

'Probably not.'

'Well please take your time and look round. Can I get you a drink?'

She didn't say anything but he understood assent from her look.

'Vodka?'

'Thanks.'

He gestured for her to go through and she went ahead. As he mixed the drinks she moved about behind his back

28]

inspecting the place then he turned and handed her her glass. 'I hate to rush things, but what's your name?'

'Alison Wonderland.'

Hood gave her a rueful little grin. 'You had me there. I thought you were going to say Annie Versary.' He held a light to her cigarette and she inhaled deeply, giving him a cool look.

'Major Breakthrough, I presume?'

'He was my uncle. I'm Ed Wake. Like the place?'

'M'mm.' She sounded doubtful, took a swallow of the drink, in perfect control. She moved two graceful steps to the window, glanced out, then ignoring him went through again towards the dressing-room. Hood said, 'Help yourself. Excuse me one minute – right back,' and stepped quickly out. In the entrance he saw the front door was unlatched, the bolt held back – she was smart! – yanked it open. The landing was empty and there was nobody on the stairs. He went back, shutting the door after him.

She was in the main room reaching for the ashtray stubbing out her cigarette, her stance full of visual grace and he thought she was very sexy and goodlooking. Hood said, 'Why don't we have dinner? There's a place round the corner where we can get the kindest cut.'

She looked down at the floor. 'I upset my drink.' He saw the stain on the carpet.

'Oh – I'll fix you another.' He turned to the drinks trolley.

'And with ice?'

'Eh? – Oh sure.' The ice bucket on the trolley was full of water. 'Get some more.' Hood carried the bucket out to the kitchen, filled it unhurriedly from the refrigerator, making a noise and giving her plenty of time, and went back. The main room was empty, so, when he strolled through, were the others.

He grinned, hoping he had played it with suitable

dumbness. His jacket lay on the chair slightly disturbed. He poured himself another drink and sat down. She had obviously come to look him over. Then his eye caught something on the carpet by the hi-fi and he went across and picked it up – a tiny dull aluminium disc. He carried it over to the light and stood looking down at it in his palm; a lens cover from a miniature Jap camera.

We-ell . . . He was impressed. She'd been clever on that. It was an unexpected touch. He hadn't noticed a thing. And now they had his picture. They weren't taking any chances. He hoped they hadn't got one of the real Conroy.

ROUGH RECEPTION

5

THE FLAT door buzzer went at nine in the morning. Hood in a robe over nothing walked through from the kitchen, saw an envelope on the mat and heard the porter's whistle going upstairs. The morning mail, by God – you got roots here faster than on the Amazon.

It was a typed foolscap envelope, Mr Edward Wake, Flat 3A and the address. Inside was a single to New York by the Panam 1.40 p.m. flight and the right-hand half of a twenty-dollar bill. It had been mailed at Charing Cross at 3 p.m. the day before, in other words just after Conroy's last phone talk at the call-box which must have been the clincher, as Gwen Mason had guessed.

Hood stuffed it in his pocket and went back into the kitchen. He had found a grapefruit, a solitary egg in the refrigerator, a packet of tea-bags and a tube of condensed milk and was making a thin breakfast. He finished the egg and a poor cup, dressed quickly and was out of the flat by 9.35.

It was a gusty morning. A flock of gulls soared over Regent's Park and he thought how little this part of London had changed since his boyhood when he had watched H. G. Wells, an old man then, taking his grim-looking afternoon walks round the Inner Circle. He turned into Baker Street Station, found a call-box and made a play of looking in the book then dialled Brady's personal number at Banner Oil.

'How is it?' Brady asked.

'I have an air ticket to New York, leaving at 1.40.'

'You have?'

'Listen, I want you to get on to the travel office and tell them I need the ticket endorsed. It's made out to Edward

Wake. I don't want to use that bogus passport and if I travel with the ticket as it is, Immigration will stop me in New York.'

'Why should they? I don't see—'

'Bill, just do this, will you? They'll stop me because the passenger list is always wired ahead and it won't have Charles Hood on it. I'm using my own passport.'

'I see.'

'You never tried taking a girl abroad for a weekend as Mr and Mrs?'

'Look—'

'O.K. O.K. I want the ticket endorsed "Charles Hood known as Edward Wake" – that's the regular formula used by all the actors, hairdressers, maybe professional dog-walkers too by now, but that's it.'

'Hold on.'

Hood held the line, watching the second-wave office workers going past.

Brady came back. 'All right, here's what you do. Walk into Cook's, Berkeley Street. It's big, busy and wide open, so it'll look natural. Go down to where they do foreign shipping passages. One of our travel people will be watching for you and he'll come up to you. Name's Stanley Clearwater, he's got red hair, snub nose, about five foot six. He doesn't work there, of course, but he's there often enough and they know him and if anybody's watching, it'll look all right. Give him your ticket and he'll fix it.'

'Fine, thanks, Bill.'

'Make it half an hour from now.'

'Did they get anything out of Conroy?'

'Not a word. And he's scared of something.'

'O.K. I want to cut.' He hung up.

Outside he suppressed the desire to walk – logically he had to keep off the streets – and caught a cab to Berkeley Street. At Cook's he saw Clearwater at once chatting

32]

animatedly with one of the staff. He walked by casually and a moment later Clearwater overtook him.

'Help you, sir?' He had bright ginger eyelashes, a brisk, smiling manner.

'I want to get this ticket endorsed.' They went through the little ploy.

'Yes, sir, certainly. If you'll just sit down there I'll have it ready in just a jiffy.'

Clearwater disappeared. Hood lit a cigarette, picked up a travel folder on the Canaries and looked absorbed. Ten minutes later, Clearwater was back, handing him the ticket in a paper folder. 'There you are, sir, all tickety-boo and Bob's your uncle. Have a nice trip.'

'Thank you, Mr Clearwater. Will you let the airline know of this detail?'

'Don't you worry, sir, I'll fix that. They'll have you by both names on their list.'

'Thank you for your trouble.'

'Just no trouble at all, sir.'

Hood gave him a grin and went out. What luck – and how rare now! – to find such joy in a man's work. It was the greatest gift you could have, better than anything, better even than a great talent. So many people hated their jobs and went on hating them and poisoning their lives.

By the time he had reached the flat again, repacked in Conroy's suitcase and left his own with the porter, it was 10.35. He timed his cab to reach Heathrow just before final check-in time and when the flight was called found himself walking out to the gate with a full crowd of something called Testament Tours. Flying the Atlantic anyway was dull enough. The film show turned out to be infantile, he finished the magazines and tried unsuccessfully to sleep. He couldn't imagine any of the Testament Tour being a tail and he sighed with relief when they arrived, even with the dreary routine of entering the home of the brave before him.

The numberless, tired, raucous, late-afternoon crowd edged slowly forward through the greenish over-used halls of Health, Immigration, Customs. At Immigration, the officer began to get tough about his 'professional name' not being on his passport but in the end waved him through.

And finally outside, bag in hand, Hood felt in spite of everything the pulse of excitement that New York always gave him – the tingle of the unexpected, the beckoning promise that at one time other places had held for him – Paris, Tokyo, Havana, Buenos Aires, but nowhere quite like this. He hated the place and loved it, found it hideous and exuberant, sometimes swore he never wanted to see it again and knew he would be back. The flight had been late, it was now six o'clock and New York was under one of the pre-summer blankets of heat. He lit a cigarette, standing at the kerb. They knew his E.T.A. Should he know what to do now?

The flow went past him. Abruptly a yellow cab swung alongside and pulled up. 'Say, bud, you change a twenty? I got all twenties tonight. Some nights it runs that way. You change that?' His out-thrust hand held a twenty bill, one of the President Jackson series.

Hood said quietly, 'L 07044504 A' – the memorized number of the half-note they had sent to him. The driver looked at him, still holding the note. He had a beat-up face. Aloud Hood said, 'I think I can change it,' dipped into his pocket and put his half against the driver's.

'Yeah,' the driver said and his eyes met Hood's. 'Was you looking for the Wake Hotel, mister?'

'The Wake, yes.'

'Get in,' said the driver, jerking his head, and as Hood slammed the door behind him the cab was already moving. Outside, they turned down to Rockaway and headed west; the driver kept his foot down, one arm out of the window holding the roof, cocky. Past the cemetery they forked towards Flatbush and Hood said, 'Where are we going?'

'You want the Wake? This is it.'

They ran through Brooklyn on Atlantic Avenue then past the intersection with Washington Avenue the driver braked and a man in a blue suit and a short-brimmed hat stepped off the kerb. He opened the door and got in. The seat crunched as he sat. Hood nodded. The man nodded back, looking him over, a big man with a mean mouth, but didn't say anything.

'What's the idea?' Hood said.

The man jerked his chin up as much as to say, We're getting there, and Hood let it ride. They took the bridge, turned up Hudson Street and were in the tangle of Lower East Side streets. From the shop signs and winos on the sidewalk, Hood guessed it was somewhere between Fourth and Canal, a rough neighbourhood. They turned a corner and pulled up, Beefy jerked his head and Hood got out.

There was a grimy brick building between a second-hand clothes shop and a bar, the driver was close up on one side of him, Beefy on the other and as they crossed the sidewalk to the entrance, Hood saw there was another man in the hallway.

'What's this?' Hood said to the driver.

'Go ahead.'

They were on the threshold of the dark scarred hall-way, obviously something unpleasant was about to happen and Hood knew he had to walk into the place or the whole enterprise was pointless. They might have laid a trap for Conroy with this as the pay-off. Conroy was a crook and crooks were always crooking each other. So this maybe was one stop before the Hudson river roped to a fruit machine.

As they went in, the third man stepped casually forward, one hand in his trousers pocket, chewing a tooth-pick. His flat simian eyes frisked Hood and Hood glanced back and saw Beefy two paces behind covering him with a revolver held close to his side. A trained gunman.

Hood had left his bag in the taxi so as to be unencumbered. Toothpick fell in alongside and they walked in silence to the end of the hall where there was a narrower passage. Toothpick jerked his chin up, indicating go on. The whole thing was professional, trimmed to essentials, no talk, no names.

The passage was dark and then everything happened at once; the driver bent at the hips, threw open a door, one of them hit Hood hard from behind with a gun-butt and as he pitched forward he was yanked inside the room like a doll and held in a necklock that nearly broke his spine.

The room swam and darkened — Hood believed he passed out for a few seconds — and he came out of it with Beefy and Toothpick systematically searching him. The man behind him, practically lifting him off his feet by his neck, was a negro who felt about seven feet tall and had Hood's head jammed into his big bushy beard. The driver was holding Beefy's gun.

The locked forearm round Hood's neck felt like the bough of a tree. Hood reached up grasping it with both hands, pulling down on it to breathe. He tried to throw his backside out, pulling down on the arms to bring the man over his head in a flying mare but the negro was backed against the wall and the driver raised the gun. Beefy stepped back and hit Hood low on the body, Hood buckled, lifted a knee with the pain and as the negro jerked him off the floor, Beefy hit him again across the mouth. Hood clung to consciousness.

The two completed the frisk, moved across the room with Hood's belongings and sat at the table looking through them. Among them they had both passports and the Conroy identity card. After a moment, Toothpick looked over and said 'O.K.' and the negro let go. Hood sagged against the wall, getting his breath, wiping his mouth and seeing the negro for the first time – an enormous bald man with a mouthful of gold teeth.

The single window of the room gave on to a brick wall and an air conditioning duct. Beyond the table was a bed. Toothpick crossed to the door, signalling to the negro, and they both went out.

'Against the wall, bud,' Beefy said, jerking the gun up. Hood didn't move. 'You hear me?' Hood retreated a pace. In about twenty minutes, Toothpick came back alone, crossed to the window and stood speaking inaudibly out of the side of his mouth to the driver. The driver nodded and went out.

'Can I get a cigarette?' Hood said, indicating his pack on the table. If he could close the distance . . .

'We're moving right now, brother.' The two came bulkily over together and Toothpick jerked his head towards the door. Hood saw the opening as Beefy's hand dropped to transfer the gun to his pocket, he shouldered in to block a guard and hit Beefy with all his strength. Beefy's teeth clicked, he went backwards with a crash, Hood caught his balance and swung away to take Toothpick's rush but Toothpick had backed off, gun out, covering him.

'Reach,' he said unexcitedly. Hood was poised, on his toes, hesitated for a second or two . . . but Toothpick meant business. Hood relaxed, slowly lifted his hands. Beefy got up on one elbow, shaking his head and blinking; he looked up and focused on Hood, furiously searched round and snatched up the gun.

'Aw, cool it!' Toothpick said. Beefy glowered and climbed sullenly to his feet. They marched out to the taxi at the kerb.

It was nearly dark. Seated between them in the taxi, Hood watched the streets, following the route and trying grimly to scheme out the probabilities. Beefy he could

[37

tackle but the other man was cool and dangerous. Go for Beefy as soon as they had the door open . . . The surroundings would give a warning – an alley, some waste lot or the riverside.

They were heading uptown and had crossed to the east side which puzzled him. Then somewhere about the east eighties the driver pulled into a space between parked cars and stopped. There were apartment blocks, people passing and across the sidewalk an illuminated sign *The Sheringham* with a uniformed negro porter under the entrance canopy. They got out. What was the idea? Hood didn't get it.

'Good evening, sir,' the porter took the bag from the driver. In a group they crossed to the entrance, waited a moment inside for the elevator then rode up to second – a smart hotel lobby with glass panelling, modern Scandinavian furniture.

'Good evening, sir,' the clerk looked up from the desk. His smile faded at the edges as he took in Hood's cut lip and the men beyond. He moved his neck uncomfortably.

Hood said, 'Conroy.'

'Yes, Mr Conroy.' The clerk consulted his list. '121, sir. You have your baggage with you, Mr Conroy? If you'd care to register—?'

'I want to get a drink and a bath. I'll fill that out later.'

'Why – uh certainly, sir.' (It wasn't regular but he wasn't going to argue, with those guys standing there.) 'Henry – 121, get the gentleman's baggage. You got it? O.K. The boy'll show you up, Mr Conroy.' His eyes were uneasy.

Hood hung there for a speculative moment. A smart blonde about thirty came out of the elevator and walked past and an older man with a stick padded by. The three mobsters were standing down the hall casually observing him and Hood had no doubt that they were going to stay below covering the entrance in case he changed ideas.

Then he stepped over to the elevator and they went up. A gentle beginning – now what?

Along the corridor above he followed the boy to the room. It was pleasant with light-toned furniture, air conditioning, the usual plastic curtains and screwed-down window.

When the boy had gone, Hood crossed to his bag and went cursorily through it. They didn't seem to have taken anything. He broke open a pack of cigarettes and took a deep drag. So here he was. So far, he knew nothing more but they obviously believed he was Conroy, otherwise why the change of decor? The rough reception had been a check-up. There was nothing to do but wait and watch his step.

He peeled his coat and turned on a bath, twirling the taps full on, took his toilet bag and cleaned up the cut lip. In the bedroom he picked up the phone and asked for room service. As he stood waiting for them to answer there was a small snap, something caught his eye and looking up he saw the door communicating with the next room open four inches.

The phone answered, 'Room service . . . Hello, this is room service . . .'

Hood held the phone away from his ear, riveted, watching the door, the voice at the other end repeating '. . . room service . . . hello . . . ?' Slowly he put the phone back, slowly stubbed the cigarette with his eyes on the door and walked carefully round the bed. The door had been opened from the other side, he gave it a gentle push and watched it swing wide.

There was a girl, a blonde, sitting with her back turned, one leg stretched out pulling her stocking up to the top of her thigh. She was in bra and mini-pants, a plumply rounded back, full bosom, a waist that pinched in over her hips. She had a cigarette in her mouth, the smoke curling up and he caught the complex mixture of

[39

her scent, her make-up creams and bottles, the intimacy
. . . a smell distantly familiar. There was a golden tan on
the inside of her thigh between the stocking top and her
pants. Then she turned and looked over her shoulder at
him.

'Good God, Miss Wonderland.'

WINDMILLER

6

F o r a second or two she sat looking at him. Then she said, 'You're late.'

Slowly she took the cigarette out of her mouth, crossed her legs, leaning her elbow on one knee and giving him a long cool look and Hood thought she had the perfect alabaster beauty of a bitch goddess – hardened by the ease with which she could get men and make them do idiotic things. This undress scene now was a little performance.

'Did we have a date?' he said.

Somewhere in the room, as he went in, a radio was playing very softly, a restrained tenor sax, 'Don't You Know I Care?' (Or 'Don't You Care to Know?') and he thought how well it fitted her. She was beautiful.

She exhaled a long jet of smoke, her dark eyelashes lowering and lifting as she looked him slowly up and down. The bra was transparent, tightly enveloping her breasts and showing the two coral-pink tips. No ugly white strips or cups – she had been getting herself an all-over tan.

'Matter of fact,' Hood said, 'I got hung up on the way here. Were they some of your friends, those salad-tossers?'

She swivelled on the stool towards the glass and he saw his money and the passports on the dressing-table. She picked up the Hood passport, turned back. 'Who's Charles Hood?'

'My name. Before it was Conroy.'

Her eyes were on him. She looked down at the passport, flipped through it, making the pages snap. 'You wouldn't make any mistake about that?'

Oddly, he had the sense of somebody listening; his eyes flicked round the room – nobody else there – to the telephone – in its cradle. Yet it was as if they were under observation.

'No mistake,' Hood said.

She stood up, dropped the passport among his other things on the dressing-table, motioning for him to take them and as Hood gathered them, she pulled on a little sepia-coloured silk robe with a T embroidered on the pocket.

'I was just ordering a drink,' Hood said. 'This was where you came in before. Care for——?'

'No thanks.' The open fold of the robe showed her thigh and the little pouch. 'We're leaving tomorrow. Please be ready at noon and no later. That's all.'

'O.K., Miss Wonderland.'

She drew on the cigarette. 'Windmiller,' she said.

'What's the T for?'

She looked faintly puzzled then said, 'Terry.'

'Come on, a drink for auld lang syne.'

Running steps drummed down the corridor outside and somebody pounded on Hood's door behind. Hood turned, eyebrows lifted. 'Here's room service, how's that?'

'The bath – hey, the bath in there!'

'Oh, my God.' Hood dashed for his room, there was the rattle of a passkey in the door as two of the hotel staff charged in. The bath was overflowing, the water swilling out on to the carpet of the room.

They turned it off, mopped up amiably – but when they had gone Hood saw the girl had shut the door. He went over and jiggled the handle but it was locked; he called out – no answer. He checked the number outside, took the phone and rang the room, the buzz came faintly through the door but she didn't answer. He dropped the phone back on to the cradle, stood considering . . . then shrugged. After all, let it lie. He wasn't close enough in yet.

He stripped, rang down for a large martini and climbed into the bath.

Forty minutes later when he walked out under the sidewalk canopy, his eye caught the grey Pontiac Grand Prix along the kerb with two men in front. A third man on the sidewalk idly turned, following him.

Hood strolled down to 70th Street, picked out a small French restaurant where he wasn't known. The menu was overblown with items like 'Delicious Royal crayfish meat taken whole from the shell, flared in vintage brandy and served with crisp morning-fresh mushrooms.' Still, it was moderately good and the Mouton Cadet '64 was superlative. He wondered how deep in the Windmiller girl was. She was a cool number – that undress act had been smart – but he thought he had caught a flash of something else when the steps had suddenly run down the corridor outside. It had gone in a second – but she was scared. Why?

Outside, the trio tailed him back to the *Sheringham*. Hood had a final drink in the bar, watching Barbra Streisand on T.V., then went upstairs, turned in and lay listening for a sound from next door. She didn't come back. He woke at three o'clock and saw the crack of light shining brightly in the dark under her door. He got up and called softly:

'Windmiller . . . ?'

A pause, then she said, 'Go to sleep.'

'Open the door.'

'No. Go to sleep.'

'Come on. A cigarette and a chat.'

'Too tired.' The light dimmed.

Hood said, 'Where are we heading tomorrow?'

'Where do you think?'

'O.K., but where do we go from? I don't get it.'

'Too bad.'

'Oh, come on, come on. We have to get down there.' Another pause. 'Guadaloupe.'

'Uh-huh.' He kept his tone mild, not very interested.

[43

Guadaloupe . . . French territory. If that was their base, he was probably going to have to fly to St Kilda's from there. He thought fast; Guadaloupe–St Kilda's ought to be an easy morning's flight in a Cessna. He stood there watching the crack under the door.

'What's the matter with you, Windmiller?'

'Nothing's the matter with me, Conroy.'

'Then why don't you open up?'

There was a longish pause, he caught the faint rustle of her movement and he could hear her breathing on the other side of the door. He waited for the click of the lock . . . Then she moved away.

'Terry . . .'

'Goodnight,' she said softly. Her light went out.

RESERVED AREA

HOOD BANKED the Turbo II Lark
Commander to starboard, surveying the
island below – the mountain at the north
dropping sharply to the sea, the green-
covered undulations of the rest, crescents
of palm-fringed beach, the sea lime-green in the shallows,
deepening to blue farther out. It looked paradise.

A yacht, like a white bird, was moored offshore. He
could see only one small built-up area near the western
shore and farther off, up the side of the mountain, a
stretch that seemed to be planted with flowers or some
bright-flowering crops. Elsewhere were a few scattered
huts. The control tower had asked for his identification
number then given him the O.K. to come in. He could
see the runway strip just inland at the south-west end.
The clock on the panel before him said 12.15.

Early the afternoon before they had caught the regular
Air France flight out of J.F.K. Airport for Pointe-à-Pitre,
the Guadaloupe airport. The flight had been full and
Terry wasn't in a talking mood. At Pointe-à-Pitre they
had found a gigantic man in a white suit named Florus
waiting for them with three coloured servants. Florus had
greeted Terry affectionately and driven them out to his
house for the night. Terry disappeared while Florus gave
Hood onward instructions.

'The aircraft is loaded and everything is ready. Instructions are very simple. You will fly out to St Kilda's
tomorrow morning on the course I have marked here,
arranging your time of arrival for twelve-fifteen. You can
pick up met. from Miami. Approach instructions are
included in the navigation file here and must be strictly
adhered to, you understand?'

'Where's Miss Windmiller gone?'

[45

Florus had pouched up his eyes. 'I advise you not to concern yourself with Miss Windmiller.'

So at six this morning, Hood had gone out to the Pointe-à-Pitre airfield, checked over the plane, a twin-engine Turbo II Lark Commander, and the freight — four unmarked crates loaded in the rear of the passenger accommodation — and two hours later Terry Windmiller had driven up with Florus and a man called Novak. Florus had watched them take off. Novak gave Hood a couple of sour looks. He was a big florid man with a lipless mouth, all over the girl, trying to make up to her. But she brushed him off and sat silent for most of the trip as if she weren't looking forward to arriving.

Now, coming in to the island, Hood lowered the undercarriage, lined up for the runway and pressed the switch for the seat-belt sign in the cabin. Minutes later they had touched down and were taxiing towards the hangar and the group of prefab huts.

Hood reckoned the runway was big enough for a full-size jet but there weren't any night-landing lights and the control tower wasn't much bigger than you had at a sports club. He switched off. The warm air came in as he opened the cockpit door. About ten men, all coloured, one in mechanic's overalls came over. The biggest, a man with a clipped moustache and a loud voice, obviously the boss, greeted Novak and the girl as they got out and threw a hand at Hood.

'Hi. I'm Clayton. You Conroy?'

'Right.' Jamaican, maybe, Hood thought, looking at his plump bossy face; sounded as if he'd lived in the States.

'Trip O.K.?' The man's eyes were hard on him.

'O.K. The magneto needs looking at and the automatic pilot goes off.'

'Yeah, well you better see that with Paley here.' He called to the mechanic. 'Paley, c'm here, c'm here — here -

46]

this is Conroy, new pilot. You get that machine inside.'

Paley nodded. Hood noticed the deference they all showed to Terry Windmiller and, as the men came over and manhandled the aircraft into the hangar, he looked round. No customs, no immigration, no sign of police, yet the island was a sovereign state. He could see no wire fence either round the airstrip. The hangar was high and wide. At the far end was a second aircraft, a de Havilland Twin Otter stripped for freight and, stacked to one side, a dozen crates like the ones he had flown in. And in this clear sunlight, the sea sparkling beyond, the breeze coming in, the quiet after the roar of the plane, the men moving about, he caught something faintly sinister.

'Hey, Conroy! C'm here.' Clayton jerked his head for him. The girl had climbed into a blue Plymouth Fury and was sitting waiting while the men piled the luggage into the car. Hood went over.

'Paley'll show you your quarters,' Clayton said. 'Get chow at the mess and I'll see you later.'

Hood nodded; he didn't think he was going to love Clayton. Clayton got in the front of the Plymouth beside Novak and they drove off. Following them with his eyes, Hood could see the tarmac road across the other side of the runway leading through groves of palms, hibiscus, coralita and canna planted on park-like grass verges, everything carefully tended. Distantly, the sea showed through a break in the trees and he saw a silver curve of beach with a row of graceful palms behind it and, landscaped in among the vegetation, a low building in white and green. It looked like a very swagger country club. Behind and beyond he made out more buildings half concealed among the trees.

'What's that along there?' he said to Paley who had drifted over.

'That's Varuna Reef.'

'Looks good, what goes on there?'

'Reserved area. You keep clear.'

Hood looked at him. 'Why?'

'Ain't for you 'n me.'

The car had disappeared. 'You want to eat?' Paley said. 'Show you your place on the way.'

They climbed into a jeep, picked up Hood's bag from the plane and Paley drove down a small dusty unsurfaced track lined with trees behind the hangar. He stopped three hundred yards along outside a small wooden bungalow. 'This is yours. I'm waitin' here for yuh.' He lit a cigarette, put his foot up.

Hood went across, shoved the door open and dumped his bag. It was a single, simply-furnished, cement-floored room with veranda at the back, shower cubicle and air conditioning and if it didn't look like Varuna Reef, it wasn't bad. He was obviously being kept close to the job; from the veranda, through the scrub and trees, he could see the hangar and one or two storage sheds. The segregation was interesting. Windmiller had got the treatment and was obviously deep in.

He called out to Paley to wait five minutes, took a quick shower and changed into a pair of tropical-weight brown check slacks, sports shirt and rope-soled shoes. The door in his hand, he looked for the key but there wasn't one. He shut it, went out and climbed into the jeep. Paley drove another fifty yards down the lane then swung left and in a few minutes they came out into a shady clearing under the high trees.

Servants were moving about between two long tables set under a roof of dried palm leaves. There was a little bar counter made of cane and leaves, a side buffet and a barbecue. Obviously this was the mess. Five or six men were at the tables eating.

'Drink?' Hood said but Paley shook his head and joined the others and Hood went over to the bar alone.

'You make a daiquiri?' he said to the barman.

'Oh, yassuh.' The barman gave him a big grin, looking happy to be asked. As he was mixing it, the Plymouth came up and Clayton, Novak and another man piled noisily out and came over, Novak in the lead. Ignoring Hood at the bar, Novak said, 'Three beers, Sam, and fast. Leave that crap. Get me three beers.'

The barman, who was cutting the lime for Hood's drink, put his knife down, wiped his hands and lifting the lid of the ice-box behind him reached in for the beer. Clayton and the other man came up. Hood stood there; he didn't say anything.

Novak turned his back on Hood, leaning on the bar and shoving out his big backside. The three were talking loudly and guffawing. When they had their beer, the barman finished Hood's drink and put the glass in front of him. Hood took a swallow, it was sharp and dry. 'Fine.'

Novak's backside came out as he sprawled farther on the bar and his elbow touched Hood's glass, Hood shifted it. Novak was obviously doing it deliberately, wanted to take the mickey out of him, establish superiority from the outset. Another guffaw from the three. Novak's elbow splayed and Hood picked up his glass again just in time. He touched Novak's shoulder. 'Mind moving over?'

'S-aay—' Novak swung round, a head taller than Hood. 'You put your paw on me?' he snarled.

'Reluctantly.'

'Yeah? You do that, you're liable to get your face pushed in.'

Quietly Hood said, 'You're annoying me and I said move over.'

'You did, did you?'

'What's chewin' you, Conroy?' Clayton put in.

'This slob Novak's giving me a pain,' Hood said.

'Jesus—!' Novak swelled, Clayton snatched his arm. 'Leave it.'

Novak glared at Hood, his face red. 'You got it

[49

coming, Conroy.' Clayton jerked his arm again and he turned back. In a moment Clayton detached himself and came round to Hood. 'While we're about it, Conroy, you got orders from me right here and now to attend to your business and anything that ain't your business don't need no attention of yours, see? You stick around the air base, your quarters and the mess here. Anywhere else, you keep out, see?' Hood nodded and Clayton went back to the others.

Hood finished his drink, went to the nearer table and sat down. They forgot him and sat down talking and laughing among themselves. They looked a rough set, he thought. The third man had a broken nose and a steam-shovel jaw and Clayton was calling him 'Big-Lunch' and 'Matza'. Mr Big-Lunch Matza, some lily. Could they be oilmen? Hood hadn't seen anything like drilling equipment yet – but secrecy and camouflage of course were the things in the oil game.

The lunch of dolphin with almonds, fried chicken and baked yams and meringue afterwards was excellent and well served. The Novak group got up and drove off. Hood finished his coffee, lit a cigarette and went over to Paley, still lounging with three others at the far table.

Indolently Paley said, 'Knock off till four.' It was apparently routine, a break in the heat of the afternoon unless something special was on.

'Fine.' Hood strolled back to the bungalow. He shut the door behind him, went through and dropped off the back veranda. At the hangar nobody was moving. There was a jeep parked in the shade. He crossed to it, released the handbrake, pushed it down the gentle slope of the road until he was clear then got in and drove off.

The road was potholed and led away from the sea through tangled bushes and mahogany trees which hid the view. This was in the opposite direction from Varuna Reef. Presently, the ground began to rise. Stretches of low broken wall appeared at the roadside and the ruins of an old stone building or two. He ran over patches of grass-grown stones where long ago the road had been cobbled. Then on the left, at a gap in the trees, there was a pair of rusty gates, one collapsed, a boarded-up kiosk and a drive-in to an area with terraces on a shoulder of the hillside. Hood pulled in and got out.

Overgrown paths ran through the place edged by broken iron railings. Then he saw that the terraces had once been pens and arenas. It was an abandoned zoo. Some of the pens had been cut in the rock, some formed artificially. Most were choked with weeds but here and there, as he went, were some that had been cleared. It had been an extensive property and must have been a showplace in its best days. How long ago – forty years, fifty? He had the picture of some family in the twenties building the place for their pleasure.

Then unexpectedly ahead, he found a row of open concrete pens with a pair of jackals in one, two wild pigs in the next, a hyena in the third. The pens, wet and dirty, didn't seem to have been tended lately – but why should animals be here at all?

The hyena was lifting its nose into the air and trotting back and forth and Hood stood there in the sun thinking how damned funny all this was. There was something about the incongruity . . . this, Varuna Reef, the whole thing, an intangible undercurrent, the sense of something furtive going on. And why thugs like Clayton, Novak and Big-Lunch Matza? Well, that was what he had to find out.

A little farther on he came to a pool covered with green slime and saw that the low surrounding railing had recently been repaired. Something in there? As he picked up a stone, a sound came from the direction of the road. He dropped the stone, went back along the path; but there was nobody at the jeep.

He drove out and swung along the road.

[51

Now he saw he was near the crest of the hill. A high wall came out of the trees on his left with the sun glinting on the green broken bottles along the top. Hood pulled the jeep under cover among the trees and got out. There must have been a sugar estate here in the old days. The planter's house had been up on the hill here behind the wall – and of course it would be the best vantage point for all the surrounding country.

He scouted along the wall, his steps crashing in the undergrowth. Parakeets screamed murder in the tree-tops. He saw two places where he could get over with risky drops from overhanging branches then found a fallen palm against the wall, climbed up and jumped down into the shrubbery on the other side.

Through the trees he saw the great house beyond like a ghost – tall arched windows, a pane here and there blazing in the sun, a chimney fallen, vegetation sprouting from the roof. It had been a handsome place of three stories built of coral stone and had stood up well to wind and weather. There had been a fine stone terrace with a balustrade and steps. He went towards it through the tall grass and made his way round the house.

Part of it was evidently still in use because through half-open shutters he could dimly perceive hangings, the dusty hint of mahogany and he had the sense of vanished families, hard business enterprise, many servants and old regrets. It must be a century old, walls two feet thick and he imagined some ancient last survivor in Bristol or Torquay who had long since forgotten the place.

The ground dipped abruptly – a former rose garden? – and he moved away from the building to skirt it. Then he came round to the front of the house and pulled up.

A two-tone green Chrysler Imperial convertible with lime upholstery was standing on the drive in front of him by the colonnaded porch. Its incongruity made a little shock. The car was at an angle and the off-side front door was wide open and there was a man at the wheel. Hood looked at him and thought who . . . ? Searching for a name. He had never seen the man before, but the face came back to him . . . from a newspaper? A chairman's report? . . . It was a man from London, a London suburban train, out of his element here – a pale oval face, short black hair, bald at the sides, the mouth slightly drawn in with the upper lip lifting to one side in a silent snarl, as if he were barely keeping his temper.

Hood racked his brains, then suddenly got it – J. D. Morell. Plastics . . . ? Packaging? The ballet enthusiast. Christ, he thought, how did Morell get into anything like this? And at this house?

Morell had not seen him but was bound to in a moment. Then a girl in a yellow dress came running out of the house.

VARUNA REEF

8 SHE RAN straight to the car. Something in her manner suggested distress. Morell snapped his head round and then she had jumped in the open front door and was standing in the car, speaking urgently to him and making a little pleading gesture with her hand. Hood couldn't hear what she was saying, but she was obviously appealing to Morell. Morell looked angry, answered shortly and waved the girl away. Hood thought he caught a sob from her. It was a strange little scene. Then a bass voice behind Hood called out, 'Hey, what you doin' there? Hey – you!'

Hood swung round. A big coloured man in a blue shirt and pants with a stick in his hand was coming up – obviously a guard. A good way behind, across the grass, another man was approaching. Hood glanced back at the car. Morell had heard the voice and seen him.

'What your business here, man?' the guard called out.

The car rolled slowly forward, the door wide, the girl still standing and holding on to the windscreen, and as the guard came up it stopped three yards away. Morell was glaring at him. The girl had turned. Hood saw it was Kim McCaine.

For a few seconds they looked at each other. There was sharp distress on her face, she was obviously in trouble; and of course, Hood thought, if she spoke in recognition of him that would be the end of everything. Mutely her eyes appealed to him; but she didn't say anything and the next moment, the guard had grabbed Hood's arm from behind.

'Who is this man?' Morell snapped from the car.

'I see him sloping round the place, suh. I dunno who

this man is. He got in here, suh, but I got my eye on him and I seen him goin' round like a cracksman, suh, goin' to break in the house.'

'That's nonsense,' Hood said. 'I'm working down at the airstrip. Just looking at the old house, that's all.'

'Your name?' Morell said.

'Conroy.'

Morell was looking at him, still and narrow – and abruptly Hood glimpsed something of another dimension in him, in the cold eyes, the bony forehead, that dark-lipped cruel mouth. It made him think of Heydrich, the Nazi 'Protector' of Bohemia and Moravia.

'What were you doing here?'

'I thought the place was abandoned. I was simply looking at it.'

Hurriedly a huge negress and a smaller man appeared in the doorway of the house beyond Morell and the car, started out – then pulled up, staring at them. Hood caught the quick turn of Kim McCaine's head as she looked away from the couple – she had obviously got away from them in the house.

Morell's upper lip lifted. 'You've been warned about keeping to your own area, haven't you?'

Hood held his stare, said nothing.

'If I find you snooping where you've got no business to be, you're in serious trouble. You understand?'

'O.K.'

'And I don't like insolence.' The narrowed eyes flicked over him. 'Now get out!'

The guard wrenched Hood's arm, Hood avoided looking at Kim McCaine and they went away across the open grass towards the trees with the guard muttering and going on about, 'You heah what Mist' Morell say, you keep off this place, man . . .' When they reached the second guard, the vociferations redoubled. The two began to get rough, jerking Hood's arm and shoving him. Hood freed himself and stopped, facing them. Quietly he said, 'Lay off or I'll bounce you. Both of you.'

They stood looking at him, sizing him up. The one with the stick said, 'You get out dis place, man, and don't you come back in. Catch you agin, that's trouble for sure. That's the way out there. Now git out, see.' He pointed down a path through the trees to an iron gate with a small gatehouse, evidently a side entrance.

Hood glanced back towards the house; it was hidden by the shoulder of the hill and the trees but at a distance he saw Morell in the Chrysler going down the drive towards the main gate. Morell was alone and he was gone in a moment.

The two men followed Hood to the gate and watched him down the lane leading away. When he was out of sight, he found the wall again and made his way back to the place where he had hidden the jeep. He climbed in, lit a cigarette. What was J. D. Morell in this? What did it signify? In those few seconds, that ordinary London face – the man from the Bodega – had seemed dangerous, capable of great evil.

He pulled out and headed down the road towards the air base, but the question kept hammering at him: Why Morell? At last something clicked in his memory . . . wait a minute . . . hadn't Morell been tied up with Regal Oil at one time? Hadn't there been . . . yes, some fishy business over an Australian deal and Morell had had to get out. He still didn't understand the yacht, Varuna Reef, the country-club aspect of the 'reserved area'; but Morell made the link with oil.

And Kim McCaine was obviously a prisoner in that house.

*

Hood spent the next morning with Paley working on the aircraft. They had dismantled the magneto and Clayton wanted more seats removed to make room for freight. Clayton was in a mood of suppressed anger and Hood guessed that Morell had told him of the encounter at the house; but either he had ordered Clayton to keep his mouth shut or Clayton was playing it his own way and had decided not to say anything yet. Clayton kept moving watchfully in and around the hangar with several other men, including a tall man named Stainburn, who ran the control tower.

All the crates in the hangar had gone. Outside, on the second road leading away from the strip, Hood noticed truck tracks. Maybe they were erecting a rig?

At 12.30 they knocked off, Hood got a lift to the mess – still deserted – and walked across to the bar counter under the palm thatch.

'Daiquiri, suh? Yassuh.' The barman gave him his big smile and turned to mix it. Hood lit a cigarette. No sign of Terry or Morell this morning. Yet from Clayton's activity, he had a feeling they were expecting arrivals.

The barman poured the drink and put it before Hood. Hood took a sip and nodded appreciatively, turned to survey the empty mess tables – and something touched his hand, a brown streak snaking out from nowhere and snatching the glass from his hand. Drink splashed him, he jerked back automatically and heard the glass smash somewhere beyond.

A burst of laughter. He looked up. Novak was standing straddle-legged in the open beyond with Clayton, Big-Lunch Matza and another man behind him. Novak had a stock-whip in his hand – a heavy lash about twenty-five feet long on a short handle and as Hood saw it lying snaked across the ground, Novak moved his arm and it rose like something alive and struck at his head. He flinched back. It exploded at his ear. Pictures of circus performers with these things flashed through his mind.

Novak moved his arm with a curious short twist and the lash reared again and bit at Hood's hand – Hood

[57

tried to snatch away – and saw it had delicately plucked his cigarette from his fingers. Novak flipped the cigarette aside, struck with the whip again and gently took Hood's sunglasses off his nose.

The group haw-hawed. The man was a virtuoso. Before Hood could retreat, the lash had risen again and coiled itself caressingly round his neck. He stood rigid – he had hardly felt it, yet if Novak had put punch behind it . . .

Lightly the coils unwound, Novak was standing with head forward, arms away from his body. The group behind was having a great time and Hood could see several of the servants looking on. He swung aside to the bar counter, searched for a weapon, the lash came over his shoulder, ripping his shirt pocket and scattering the contents. He snatched up a chunky glass ashtray and, jumping forward, threw it hard – but before he could duck away, the lash had jerked his leg from under him and he fell heavily.

For a moment he stayed down, his thoughts racing. Hood knew that Novak had him beaten unless he could get cover or close the range but for each step he moved nearer, Novak retreated. Novak could take an eye out – blind him with a single smash. He got up, jumped for the nearest table and took the whip painfully on the shoulder. He skimmed a plate hard at Novak then another. The first was wide, the second sailed for Novak's head, and when Novak ducked Hood was up with a chair in front of him, running forward.

Novak's whip arm moved and the lash tore the chair from Hood's grasp and threw it aside, but then Novak was stepping back and jerking at the whip handle, trying to disengage the lash.

Hood dived to the table, swept up a glass water carafe. He swung it by the neck, feinted to make Novak duck again – and slung it sideways with all his strength. Novak had bobbed upright again, the whip now free; the carafe – a lucky shot – caught him glancingly on the neck and going backwards, Novak tripped and fell.

As Hood belted towards him, the three others stepped quickly in the way. 'O.K., Conroy.'

'Keep out of this!' Hood said.

He dodged to pass but Clayton and Matza dived in and grabbed him.

'Keep out of it!'

'O.K. – you hear?' They held him and Hood, looking down, saw Clayton had a razor. They shoved him away, releasing him and stood there silently, eyes on him, while behind them Novak got to his feet spitting and wiping his mouth with the back of his hand. He had a cut chin and he looked blue murder at Hood.

'Get back to your drink,' Clayton said, jerking his head to Hood. Hood was tense, suppressing the itch to go for him. He said, 'O.K. I'll have this one on Novak.' He turned and walked back, picking up his sunglasses, cigarette pack and lighter.

'Yassuh?' It seemed to Hood that there was a beam of new appreciation in the barman's grin.

*

After lunch, Hood collected a towel from the bungalow and walked down to the beach. As he reached it he heard a deep zoom to seaward and saw one of the powerboats carving a white streak across the blue towards the yacht. Shading his eyes, he made out Morell in the stern with Clayton and another man. That took care of them for a while.

He moved into the shade of the palms and kept going. The sky was white with the sun. The sea made a gentle lapping but farther out it boomed from the reef. Presently the beachside shrubbery grew thicker and wilder, the palms closer together, some of them sweeping their trunks out over the sand. The sand was hard and white, without a trace except the faint triangles of birds' feet, the palm-leaves made shifting patterns over it and the shallows of the sea were pale green. Now and then little red-back crabs scuttled across his path.

Hood hid the towel among the shrubs, marked the spot and struck inland. There were grape vine, mahogany and flamboyant trees, and after about twenty minutes of hard going among the undergrowth he saw a clearer area ahead. Going more cautiously, he moved up and saw two long wooden sheds in a clearing, three or four smaller huts and piles of unassembled prefabs.

Camouflage netting strung from the trees with bits of foliage on top extended over the two main sheds and he could see power lines leading in from a transformer. What the hell was this?

Keeping under cover, he scanned the area. Three or four trucks were parked beyond the big huts but there was nobody about. Cautiously he moved round until he was opposite the huts, stepped out and jolted – two men were lying on the ground about twenty feet away with straw hats over their eyes. Hood retreated, moved along a little, stepped across the open space and turned the angle of the nearest hut. There was a door with an open padlock on the hasp; he eased the door and went in.

The place smelt of dust and packing, crates were stacked along the sides and in the middle was a long pile of machine parts. Hood tiptoed over to them – closed metal cylinders with pipe connections, several retorts and drums and something like a half-assembled still.

Some of the pieces had the heavy look of equipment made fifty years ago and the handling surfaces were worn from use. His eye caught a mark and he bent closer – it was the cyrillic letter Ж.

Slowly, reflectively, Hood straightened up – a distant bell ringing in his mind. It was something he had seen before, something even familiar . . . and yet he couldn't

60]

get it. He stood trying to recall, but it didn't come. Farther along he saw a metal inscription plate on a cylinder, the sort of plate that makers put on old-fashioned machinery. It was rubbed and he had to peer closely to make it out. *L'Arlésienne. Marque déposée. F. Dumont et fils. Lyon et Nice. Fabricants de batteuses, extracteurs et autre matériel pour* ... The rest of the plate had been torn away.

What in God was a *batteuse* or an *extracteur*? What did they beat or extract? From the crates, this was evidently the equipment he had flown in but it was nothing to do with oil. He was baffled.

A sound made him turn quickly – a shadow moved across the filtered sunlight at the door. Hood dropped to the ground under cover of the machinery. Somebody came in. He lifted his head and saw a man in overalls inside the shed looking round, muttering to himself. He took a few steps in Hood's direction then turned and went out. Hood prayed he wouldn't padlock the door; the windows were fixed.

He gave it a minute then rose and ran on tiptoe along the hut. The door was open about a foot, he could see the man's ankles under it and caught the tang of a cigarette. Presently the ankles disappeared. Hood was about to push the door when the man coughed, a few feet away.

Hood cursed. He waited five minutes, hearing nothing, then gently eased the door and stepped out. The man was standing twelve feet away, back turned. As Hood edged away, the man had a spasm of coughing and Hood turned the corner of the hut and sprinted across the open to the trees. He ducked under cover and turned to watch.

Now he could see two more men walking slowly round the perimeter like a patrol, then a dog bounded out of the bushes and frisked round them. Hood stood there but the two were coming towards him and reluctantly he turned away and headed for the beach.

The spot where he had left the towel was two hundred yards back. He stripped off shirt and pants and went naked into the blinding shimmer of the sea. Everything was sea and sky. He swam out, turned back and lay on the beach, smoking and waiting. Just before sunset he saw the motor boat leave the yacht and return to the jetty.

He stood up, brushed the sand off and dressed, buried the towel and headed down the beach towards the 'reserved area' of Varuna Reef. Some low scrub gave him cover going past the hangar area. At the jetty he counted four boats.

Farther on was the main Varuna Reef building with glass walls, lawns, a pool, smart basket chairs and parasols on the apron, a stand of sea-fishing rods. Lamps were lit and he glimpsed a servant or two in white moving about a wide low-ceilinged lounge open on two sides to the air, with modern screens, low tables and sculpture.

The feather palm-heads floated above, their trunks weaving as if they had been arranged by some inspired gardener and Hood, who had seen a few smart places, knew he was looking at something special. Riches from somewhere had hit St Kilda's, for whoever had built this had power.

It was nearly dark now and there was no wind. Everything that had moved incessantly during the day, the trees, the sea, the grass, the bushes, the sky, was still and quiet. The day had burnt them out, exhausted them. The sky and the sea seemed vaster. The sea crept with a small lapping.

Hood made to move on, then ducked down. A group of four figures was coming along the beach. They were spread in line and were holding rifles across their chests ready to shoot and they moved their heads, scanning the shore. A beach patrol! Flattening in the scrub, Hood crawled for thicker cover and lay still. He hoped to Christ they hadn't got dogs. In a minute he heard one of them say something. They were going by.

He lay there without moving until it was quite dark, then raised his head. Other lights were on among the trees. He got up and walked across towards them. The tarmac road wound among the trees with a scattering of white cottages set back across the grass, most of them in darkness.

It was warm and the air was sweet with night blossoms. The few lamps along the road left pools of darkness. Intermittently he could hear the shrill of whistling frogs and then far off behind him in the stillness the sound of an islander's flute.

He followed the road round, keeping to the verge. Abruptly he made out a car, a big convertible parked in the dark with the lighted shutters of a house up the gentle grassy rise beyond. Morell? He approached, but before he could avoid it, slipped into a deep rain ditch half concealed by the overgrowing poinsettia shrubs. The dead undergrowth in the ditch made a hell of a noise under his weight. He climbed back out as fast as he could and ducked down. A light shone out from the house as if somebody was looking out, then went again.

Hood moved forward. He skirted the house, finally found the way over the ditch and went silently across. A cascade of bougainvillaea hid one corner, he picked his way round it and stepped on to the terrace, dimly lit from inside. Somebody moved in the deep shadow in front of him. He froze.

The figure stepped out – Windmiller. She was in a slim silver lamé top, darkly gleaming, with narrow black silk sleeves, evening pants, her hair up. He could smell her scent. She held a revolver on him.

'What are you after?' she said.

'What am I after? That's a hell of a question, Windmiller.'

[63

'Keep back. Why have you been prowling round here?'

'You know, this is the richest conversational exchange we've had for days. Can I tell you you're looking lovely?'

'What are you doing here?'

'I was hoping for a neighbourly drink. We could get the one we didn't have in London or New York.'

'You are not funny.'

'Come on. You owe me a long friendly chin-wag. Morell can wait.'

'I don't think you understand what you're saying.'

'What do you do in this set-up?'

'Don't you know?'

'No.'

Her face was dramatized by the shadow – the perfect hollows of the eyes under her dark eyebrows, the line of her cheek, the small indentations at the side of her mouth. She was cool and lovely, he thought.

She snapped, 'Turn round.' Hood turned. 'Go down there – to the car.'

He went down the drive-way to the convertible, hearing the rustle of her movement behind him. 'Get in,' she said.

Hood got in, she came round the other side. It wasn't Morell's car, evidently her own. She had put the gun away and slid in behind the wheel. He said nothing, sitting half-turned towards her, seeing her sultry profile against the night as she started the car and moved it without lights down the drive and on to the road.

She drove slowly and presently swung off between some palms down a dip to the beach. She switched off the engine, got out and walked round to the front of the car. Hood followed her. He put a light to her cigarette and they stood leaning against the car looking out over the sea with the moon coming up.

'Why don't you tell Morell you found me scouting around?' Hood said.

'What makes you think I won't?'

Hood drew his breath in mockingly. 'Tomorrow morning, after a rousing night, over breakfast?'

'My business,' she snapped and he was a little astonished at his lucky hit.

'What's the matter?'

'Nothing's the matter,' she said.

'Yes, there is, You're scared for one thing. What are you scared of?'

'You're mistaken.'

'O.K.'

They smoked in silence for a minute. She said, 'Are you a detective?'

'What? My name's Conroy.'

'You're not Conroy.'

Hood said, 'Don't be crazy. Where did you get that idea?'

'Conroy'd know better. He wouldn't be so interested in things that weren't his business.'

'You have it wrong, Windmiller.'

'Have I?'

'Yes.'

'Morell saw you at the house up there yesterday. And you were snooping here tonight.'

'Yes, what goes on up there? Who is that girl?'

'Keep your nose out!' She exhaled cigarette smoke, not looking at him and there was a hint of contempt in her manner. 'Get out of here. Go away.'

'Why?'

'You don't know what you're mixed up in.'

'Suppose you tell me?'

'I'm telling you to get out – while you can.'

'But you forget they just hired me.'

Vehemently she swung on him. 'They're going to kill you as soon as they find out you're not Conroy – don't you see that, you fool?'

'So who am I supposed to be?'

'Charles Hood, whoever he is. Not Conroy.'

'You have it confused.'

Suddenly she flared, 'Can't you understand, if Morell suspects, you've got no chance! I mean *no chance*. You've seen these men. These people are killers. Morell will kill you and it will be horrible. He'll tear every last fact out of you before he lets you die.'

There was a pause. Hood looked at her. 'You ought to give me that gun then . . . h'm . . . ?'

She stood there in silence for a long time then abruptly she threw away the cigarette, reached into her bag and took the gun out. She handed it to him, a snub .38. 'You didn't get it from me.'

'Of course I didn't.' He slid it into his pocket. 'Now tell me what they're doing here?'

She turned her head away, not answering. The sea shone in the moonlight. The palmheads were black against the sky. Everything was very quiet.

'Terry.'

No answer.

'What's Morell's part? What is all this — Varuna Reef and so on?'

'I don't know.'

'You do, come on.'

'I don't know, I tell you. *I don't know!*'

It was a lie but he didn't have the heart to press her. He stood looking at her, at the faint light on her hair, the outline of her lips and her neck. And suddenly he pulled her to him and kissed her, felt her arms begin to hold him and then she was fighting him, fighting away, freed herself and hit him hard across the face.

'Damn you! Go away, go away. Leave me alone. Why did you come here?'

'Why did you come?'

He caught her again, pulled her close, she hit him again and struggled, fighting him off and then suddenly

66]

she yielded and her arms were round him, her body yielding to him, pressing against his, the fingers of one hand on the back of his neck as he held her in a long kiss. She broke away, catching her breath, 'Charles . . . don't, darling . . .'

He felt her hands digging into him. He said, 'We could go places together. When I've finished something here.'

She tried to tear herself away but couldn't, put her forehead to his chest and in a whisper she said, 'There's an empty hut . . . along there.' He looked along the moonlit beach and saw the small hut of palm branches among the trees.

'Safe there?'

She nodded. They turned, hardly looking at each other, electricity between them. Hood felt the tautness of his skin, the small tremor of muscles, the shrinking in his chest. The beach, the trees, the moonlit sea vanished and only Terry beside him existed as they went to the hut.

Inside was a splash of pale moonlight. He had her in his arms and her cool mouth was on his, her lips open, her body moulding with his, her arms pulling him to her with desire. Holding her in the kiss, he began unfastening her clothes. She broke away gently, 'Darling—' sank down and pulled him down to her. He kissed her neck and her breasts and said, 'Take your clothes off.'

Silently she drew him to her, searching for him and finding. She lifted her loosened bra and, bending, pressed him close against her breasts and then bent her head and kissed him, withdrawing and enveloping him again until he moved, lifted her chin and made her lie down.

She shuddered at his penetration; and when he was inside her, she lay with small intakes of breath as if she dare not move, he closed her mouth with kisses and then he felt her soaring away, gripping his shoulders with arching fingers and everything in him was flying irresistibly with her.

They lay still in the warm gloom of the hut. She shifted at last and bit his arm. 'Darling . . . It was so good.' He kissed her nude shoulder, his hand moving over her middle, her long thighs. In a little while she was lying on him.

He released her and she moved down over him as if she couldn't get enough of him. He lifted her up and in a moment they both lay as if a small movement would bring the climax, Hood holding her hard as her small inner spasms drove him wildly to the edge and then they couldn't hold back any more and together were skimming off the rim of the world.

It was quiet in the hut. Far off they could hear a dog barking from some village, then another started up, then a third. Presently they lit cigarettes and lay smoking, watching the complex and slowly shifting pattern of light and the stars through the decaying roof. She said, 'Nobody's ever made love to me like that before. Now I know I've never really . . . oh, half, but nothing like that, God.'

'Well, it's luck. Works with some, not with others. And it's the occasion too.'

She was stroking his belly. 'God, I really lost my head. I suppose plenty of women go through their lives not feeling anything like they should.'

'Well, with some men it seems it's a one-sided affair – only their side and that's what makes it go wrong. You know . . . there's a subtle and special importance in the way a man makes the girl feel that his domination and tigerish possession of her is carrying her up, is *for* her, *with* her – not just a bit of goatery by him. As soon as he lets her feel he's not with her, then it's no good for her.'

She kissed him.

Hood said, 'I believe in a girl audibly expressing her enjoyment too – naturally, not like a fire-engine; but you get a girl who lies there going through it silently, almost politely, and maybe gives a little squeak or a whimper when she goes off bang – takes away half the pleasure.'

'Do they?'

'Oh, God, some girls come and you can hardly damn well tell – not a hiccup.'

'Maybe you haven't been trying?' She grinned.

'Maybe I haven't now?'

She nibbled his ear and said very softly into it, 'Do you know when I come?'

Hood reached and took her cigarette, stubbed it in the sand and stubbed his own out. He kissed her and they made love again and she strained him to her, pulling her into him and moving with his movements. Afterwards she got up and put her clothes on. He watched her then dressed too. She said, 'It's late. I must go back.'

'To Morell?'

'Charles, don't – I—'

Abruptly the mood had changed and she turned urgently to him. 'You've got to get out of this place. No – no, don't – and don't ask me any more. Go away, I'll meet you somewhere as soon as I can but don't stay here, darling. Not now.'

'Haven't I a small claim to know why?'

'Because Morell will see, for one thing. That's enough. You don't know what he's like, he's cold and deadly, he'll kill you. What happened this morning? You were in a fight or something?'

'With Novak. Have you seen him use that whip?'

She nodded. 'He used to be a circus act. And he had animals.'

An animal trainer. It was the bizarre note again – and then as he stood looking at her in the dimness of the hut

[69

there was a sound outside. She caught his arm and they stood very still.

'Beach patrol,' she whispered. 'Charles, stay here.'

He caught her and pulled her close, lifted her head and kissed her fiercely. She disengaged herself.

'Don't come with me. Stay here till I start the car – they can't do anything to me. As soon as you hear the car, go into the trees behind here and to the left. Keep off the beach.'

She stepped into the patch of moonlight at the door and disappeared.

LOVE ON SKATES

9

AT EIGHT o'clock next morning, immediately after breakfast, Clayton pulled up at the hangar in a jeep. 'Hey, Conroy, c'm here.'

Hood walked over, wiping his hands on cotton waste.

They had had a row the night before when Clayton and Matza had driven up to the bungalow just as he got back and wanted to know why he hadn't been on the job that afternoon. Hood had played him off and said Paley had been there anyway. Clayton had blown up and been threatening. They had to have one aircraft ready to fly at any time – and Hood had better watch his step.

Now from the jeep, Clayton said, 'How long you got on that engine?'

'I told you last night, about an hour.'

'You got stores to pick up at Pointe-à-Pitre. Get your gas ready to take off and wait till I give you the O.K.'

Hood nodded curtly. Clayton swung the jeep, kicking up dust. But it wasn't until Hood was walking back to the bungalow after lunch that Clayton, who hadn't appeared at the mess, overtook him. 'O.K., Conroy. Get going right away. When you get there, see Florus and he'll have the stuff loaded. I want it back here by tomorrow forenoon.'

'All right.'

'And no mistakes, uh?'

'Absolutely,' Hood said.

As it was, they had taken out insurance against mistakes. Hood found the aircraft in the open and as he stowed his gear inside, Novak and Big-Lunch Matza came up, humped in overnight bags and climbed into the passenger compartment. The escort.

Clayton was looking on. When Hood was ready, he taxied to the runway, got the O.K. from Stainburn and took off. As they climbed, he looked down on the island, picking out the big house on the hill, the old zoo, the buildings and beach at Varuna Reef. The camouflage over the huts was remarkably effective and he couldn't locate the place with any certainty. There was nobody outside the big house but one of the powerboats was moored in a little bay beyond Varuna Reef – somewhere he hadn't seen yet. The fields of flowers up the mountainside puzzled him; they must be some crop for livestock which only grew up there.

He headed the plane out over the sea. The flight was routine. Novak and Matza played gin rummy all the way. At Pointe-à-Pitre, three of Florus's men were waiting to take charge of the aircraft and when Hood had cleared through Customs and Immigration, Florus's driver came forward beyond the barrier. 'Good evening, suh. Evening.'

Hood couldn't help thinking how smoothly it all worked. They had everything laid on, they were beautifully organized and it was going to be difficult to trip them on anything important. Novak and Matza slapped the driver's back and guffawed heartily apparently glad to be back in Guadaloupe.

They all walked outside to a green Citroën near the airport entrance. It was a busy spot, bustling and noisy with local people and departing travellers – women with bright headcloths, skinny porters, cotton-shirted men with canes, barking and gesticulating, mighty dames swaying at their moorings like battleships. Vehicles were swinging past on the road with the extra dash and noise that they always seemed to have on French territory.

The driver bent inside the back of the car arranging something, Novak and Matza stood waiting. Hood went round the stern to get in by the near-side door, then, as he paused to let a truck zoom past, somebody charged him hard in the back.

Pitched forward, he threw out an arm, partly blocked his momentum on the corner of the Citroën before his hand slid off and the high truck wing gave him a glancing jolt that swung him sideways off his feet. There was a hiss of brakes, and in three blank seconds Hood landed against somebody and sprawled.

Cautiously he picked himself up. Two or three people whom he had been thrown among were exclaiming, a young man was getting to his feet. Hood was dusty, his right wrist felt limp but otherwise he was all right.

'Suh, suh – you all right, suh?'

'What you foolin' at, Conroy?' Matza snarled.

'What happen, suh?'

'I don't know. Somebody shoved me.' Hood straightened up, flexing his elbow and over the head of the small gathering caught sight of Novak standing unconcerned by the car. He had a look of sarcastic amusement and Hood understood.

The truck driver had got down and was joining in the explanations. Obviously the locals wanted to get the most they could out of it but Hood said, 'Ça va. Ce n'est rien.'

'Sweet Jesus, let's get outa here,' Matza said.

Blocked cars were tooting behind. Hood checked back – nobody in the group seemed hurt. They piled into the car and in a moment were clear, swinging out of the airport compound and picking up speed along the road to the town. Novak was sitting with the driver. Matza was muttering moodily to himself, staring out of the window. Hood massaged his wrist.

The warm late afternoon air, the leafy smells of the Caribbean came in through the window. The sky was turning a rich yellow, there was the greenery of plantations and gardens on either side, a splash of bougainvillaea here and there on walls and rusty corrugated iron roofs, the hills behind. The road ran past small unpainted wood houses and shops with signs in French. Women balancing high loads on their heads stepped off on to the verge to watch them pass, talking to themselves and chuckling.

Florus's house, where they had spent the night on the outward journey to St Kilda's, was a fine grotesque piece with fretwork trimmings and white wood knobs all over. Florus greeted them on the veranda. Hood drew a room on the first floor and when he had showered and changed, got one of the servants to bind up his wrist. Downstairs, he found Florus and the other two on the veranda with drinks.

'And what would you care for, Conroy – tequila, whisky, schnapps? We have everything.' Florus held his gold-knobbed cane between his knees, sitting in a great wicker chair.

'A martini,' Hood said.

'Excellent. Jalot makes the best martini in the West Indies. I hear you had a mishap – I trust you are not hurt?'

'No, it wasn't much.'

'One of them voodoo tricks,' Novak said and laughed. Hood took a chair and Florus leaned forward. 'You can leave by seven tomorrow morning. They will have the plane loaded and fuelled, everything prepared. We can't afford delay.'

'Sure.'

Hood's drink came, Florus sat talking about local superstitions. After a while, Novak and Big-Lunch got up and walked into the house and a moment later, Florus excused himself to give an order.

Hood looked round. The servants had momentarily disappeared. Tomorrow morning and the flight back to St Kilda's was one thing but he didn't fancy an evening in the gentle company of Novak and Matza, probably gin rummy all night. He went quickly down the veranda steps into the garden to the deep shadows under the palms, walked down the drive to the last of the parked cars and got in. He started the engine, ran down the drive without lights and swung out on to the road. As he trod down, flicked the headlights on and the car leapt forward he caught a shout from the veranda behind.

The car was another Citroën and went like a bird. Hood didn't know the way into town but guessed luckily and was soon among the streets of small arcaded shops and houses with balconies. He glimpsed a promising bar with a little lighted menu card up outside, pulled up and backed to the place. The street wasn't very well-lit and he parked the Citroën under a tree. The bar had low lights, only two other couples in the corners, a pick-up was playing very softly 'Poor Butterfly' and Hood thought the place looked fine.

At the bar he hitched up on one of the stools and ordered a martini. He lit a cigarette and exhaled the smoke with a sigh of relief at being away on his own; and when the drink came he sat with his mind going over the unexplained facts, the activity on the island, which he simply did not understand.

Why had Terry Windmiller told him to get out. Why was she so scared? And now why the haste to get the stores back? He finished the drink and asked for another.

The barman put the fresh martini before him, Hood took a sip and in the mirror over the bar caught Novak's face coming in from the street. Big-Lunch Matza was right behind him. They both looked hard in Hood's direction, then slid in behind one of the tables near the door.

Hood groaned inwardly at the prospect of a ruined evening. Novak had a big cigar going and looked very cocky; his face under his yellow hair was flushed pink. As the waiter went up to them, Novak said in a loud voice, 'We wanna take our time. Maybe we wanna eat big but right now we want two good fat bottles of beer. You got some good beer?'

Hood put his glass down and cursed. Then he did a double-take at the man who had come through the service door at the other end of the bar. The man was suddenly beaming, arms extended.

'Ernesto!'

'Charles, my God. What in hell are you doing in Guadaloupe?'

'What the hell are *you* doing in Guadaloupe?'

Ernesto was a chunky thirty-five with a broad, good-looking, humorous face and pencil moustache. They hugged each other, joyfully pounded each other's back. Hood had known Ernesto Estiribbia years before in Paraguay where they had been great and good friends and it had been a long time since they had seen each other. Ernesto, who had gone through two fortunes, had been one of the great *noceurs* of Latin America.

'What happened to Paraguay?'

Estiribbia's forehead corrugated, he gave a long slow shrug, smiling. 'You know, Asunción, it is not so good now. La politica. So I come here.'

'Well, if you're looking for good politica, boy, you're looking for something. What are you doing?'

'This,' Ernesto spread his hands. 'This place is mine — drinks, a little good food. It is a pleasant climate. Life is easy-going. I make out. Of course, it is not so much fun as the old days . . . But you tell me where is it as much fun.'

'What about Las Palomas, what happened to that?'

'Oh, I brought it here, but—'

'What! Ernesto — you run that old corrida here?'

'Oh, it is not the same. I started to make it the same for the Americanos, the visitors, I thought it would be funny, but the police, they make trouble. The French, they do not laugh much now. Very solemn now.' He laughed.

76]

Hood gazed at him, struck by inspiration. Las Palomas dance-hall had been one of the glories of Asunción and here . . . 'Is Maria still with you? I suppose she can't be . . . after all . . .'

'Oh God, she is magnificent,' Ernesto's eyes rolled upward. 'Better than ever. Sometimes for fun we have a private evening. Members only.'

Hood glanced up into the mirror at the table by the door. Novak and Big-Lunch were deep in conversation. Hood became urgent. 'Look, Ernesto, can you put on the old thing tonight, if I bring somebody? As a great favour?'

Estiribbia shrugged, looked doubtful. 'You know, they close me down . . .'

'Come on, Ernesto, for the hell of it. Just once.'

Estiribbia poured himself a whisky and water. He took a drink, gave Hood a rueful smile. 'Sure – we do it. To hell with the police. Give me a little time, say in an hour. You want to eat here?'

'Fine. Can you get another girl for me?'

'Yes. What do you want, blonde, brunette?'

'A brunette.'

'O.K. I will fix everything while you have dinner.'

'Ernesto, you're a hero. Now look, come here . . . the man on the right there, yes, the big bull . . . yes . . .'

Hood ordered papaya, Spanish omelette and salad and a Blanc de Blanc. They gave him a little table near the bar and he saw that Novak and Matza had ordered food too. Novak was guffawing, kept calling the waiter over and looked in the mood for trouble. As Hood finished, a girl came in through the service door and sauntered over, smiling. 'Hello—'

Hood was on his feet.

'Ernesto said you were here,' she said.

'Please sit down and have a drink.'

She was dark and pretty and carried the situation off

with perfect naturalness. She was called Josée and as she sat drinking her coupe of champagne and they talked, Hood could hear Novak arguing with the waiter about girls, getting noisier. He wanted a girl too. Finally, when Hood had paid, he stood up. 'Let's go somewhere and dance.'

'Oh, yes.' She gave him a lovely smile. 'I like to dance.' Novak had caught the words.

'Do you know of a good place?'

'M'mm.' They went towards the door and as they reached the other table, Novak said in a loud voice, 'You wanna dance, Big-Lunch? C'mon, man.'

Hood stopped, looked down at him. 'Why don't you beat it, Novak?'

'Who me? I wanna dance. C'mon, Big-Lunch.' They edged out after Hood and the girl. Hood saw their Citroën drawn up behind his. As he started the car, the girl said a little worriedly, 'I don't like that man. He's going to make trouble.'

'Don't worry.' Behind them, Novak flicked headlights as an irritant.

Hood pulled out, driving carefully to the girl's directions, and ten minutes later they sighted the entrance to Las Palomas. Hood parked and they walked across. They could hear Novak's bellow coming up behind and Matza laughing and Hood felt the slight constriction in his chest that he had when he badly wanted to slug somebody.

They paid at the cash desk with the beat of a band thudding out, went through a red-carpeted foyer and turned into the full blare of the hall – a big well-lighted place, green walls, high ceiling, the band zipping it out on the rear platform, a big, mirrored globe dangling from the ceiling slowly revolving and about twenty couples dancing, with others sitting out. A fancy mirror-faced staircase wound up from behind the band and the whole thing looked so wonderfully sedate, Hood couldn't help a laugh.

'You have been here before?' the girl said.

'Yes – not in Guadaloupe, though.'

'I think it is very nice.'

'Well, don't let it mislead you. You know the special thing . . .?'

'Special thing? No.'

'You *don't*? Well, come on.' The band was playing and they went out on to the floor. She danced beautifully and Hood said, 'You've got a talent for movement, Josée.'

She gave him a smile and held him. Hood was watching Novak and Matza taking in the place from the sidelines. He said, 'Listen, Josée, when he starts, follow me, will you?'

'How do you mean?'

'The man from the bar over there. Here it goes – watch.'

A lovely girl was sauntering in Novak's direction, a tall bosomy brunette with dark eyes, creamy teeth and dangling ear-rings, her hair down to her shoulders, very short skin-tight skirt moulding her thighs, belly and derrière. She gave Novak a flicking, wide-eyed, innocent look – better than the slinkiest come-on, and Hood said admiringly, 'My God, she is better than ever. Glorious girl.'

'Do you know Maria?'

'Used to. You sure you don't know this thing?'

'No.'

'Well, watch her. She's asking him if he wants to dance.' Maria was speaking to Novak and the next minute Novak was leading her to the floor. He looked dazed.

'Can't believe his luck,' Hood said, chuckling. 'Hardly dare touch her.'

'What's so funny?'

'The anticipation.' Hood was shaking silently.

Novak and the girl were in among the other dancers and in a minute her lovely face was close to his and she was whispering in his ear.

'Now she's asking him if he wants to come upstairs with her.'

Novak had changed colour, looking at the girl. They saw him nod, open-mouthed. The two danced a little more then the girl steered Novak to the staircase behind the band and, breaking off, they climbed up. Everybody could see them.

Hood cast round. 'Quick, follow me,' and pulled Josee after him through a door to a flight of service stairs. At the top he had another moment of uncertainty finding the door Ernesto had said he would find, then they were through into a small, bare, dimly-lit room. The light came through a glass wall panel from the room next door which was dominated by a big bed. They could see it all clearly.

'But how——?'

'One-way glass. Watch,' Hood said. At that moment, Maria came in next door followed by Novak. She bolted the door behind them and they heard her say, 'Would you like to make love, you big beautiful boy?'

A gasping gurgle came from Novak.

'Well, you take off al lyour clothes. And I'll take off all mine.'

Novak took off coat, shoes, socks, shirt. He couldn't tear his eyes away from the girl who was slowly and enticingly stripping. She was in black stockings and black lace underwear. Slowly she unclipped her stockings, peeled them. Novak seemed to be dry in the mouth, was wetting his lips and breathing hard. She put a hand behind her back, her bra came loose and she shrugged it off.

Softly Hood said, 'Honey pie. Isn't she terrific?'

Her oval breasts stood out, the light golden nipples making their own sweet prolongation.

'Melons for delight.'

Maria dipped out of the panty-girdle, a rich swell of hips and dark triangle.

'Oh, God.'

Novak tore out of the rest of his clothes. 'And bejasus,' Hood said, ''tis as thick as a swan's neck!'

Novak came a step forward, grabbed for Maria, but she held up a hand, knees crooked. 'Wait! Wait – please!'

'W-what is it?' Novak's voice shook.

'I've got a special thing . . . you know . . . about roller skates.'

Novak gagged, '. . . roller . . . ?'

'It's so wonderful! . . . Wonderful . . . Will you, honey bear . . . ?'

'Uh?'

'Put on that pair of skates there . . .'

Bewilderedly, Novak cast about. Then he darted aside, bent down and they saw him feverishly strap on a pair of roller-skates. He stood up! He was in high form.

'Now, honey-bud,' Maria said. 'You stand over on that side of the room, I'll go over here, back to the wall, open my – legs – and – oh—'

Novak, eyes half-shut, gave a sort of wince.

'—you come at me full-tilt. Oh, it's terrific. Yes?'

Novak nodded, voiceless.

As Maria retreated, leant back against the far wall, Novak backed off with the skates. 'Ready?'

'Uh.'

Suddenly she said, 'Now!' Novak surged forward like a battering ram, flashed towards her. At the last second, she flipped aside, Novak hit the curtain behind her, went through and vanished.

'Here!' Hood yanked Josée across to a spyhole and looking down they were just in time to see Novak fly out from the bottom of a chute, naked, erect and on roller skates – in the middle of the ballroom.

A warning bell had stopped everybody dancing and they were all standing expectantly watching.

A voice on the speaker said, 'Look who's here.'

*

*

When Hood woke it was still dark but he could see the first red streak of dawn low down at the open window. He checked his watch – 5.30, got up and dressed quickly.

He had stayed late, after the dance-hall scene, at Ernesto's apartment before returning to Florus's. Ernesto knew nothing of the island group but when Hood had mentioned Florus his grin had faded. Florus was dangerous and had heavy protection – not a man to be trifled with. Hood had told him that he was going out to the airfield early to look at the freight and they had arranged for Ernesto's driver to pick Hood up near Florus's house at 5.30.

Hood snapped his grip shut and went downstairs. The house was quiet and in the dimness he made out a man stretched sleeping across the front veranda. Hood tiptoed to the rail, climbed over and dropped softly on to the grass. He ducked down, hearing the man stir. Three minutes later he was out of the drive walking rapidly along the street.

There was the dampness of heavy greenery in the air and at the corner he saw the gleam of Ernesto's white station-wagon in the ground mist. The driver greeted him with a big grin and switched round in his seat with a package.

'M'sieur send this, say present for you.'

Hood unwrapped the paper; there were three sticks of plastic explosive and a clutch of time pencils. A note with them said, 'Souvenir from Asunción. You never know.' Hood grinned. Ernesto had been an enthusiastic revolutionary *plastiqueur* in Asunción and Hood could imagine him packing the plastic with a glint of envy. He stuffed the package under a shirt in his grip and said to the driver, 'Bon. Allons-y.'

On the way to the airport, the sun thundered up. Sending the driver back, Hood checked through the

Administration block and found the aircraft two hundred yards beyond where they had left it the evening before. Two men in overalls lounging on a fork-lift eyed him as he approached. Hood went round the nose, climbed up to the cabin. They had already refuelled the aircraft and the clip for the cargo manifest was gone. As he turned aft into the accommodation, the rear door opened.

'What you want, Missieu?' It was one of the overalled pair.

'I'm the pilot.'

'Missieu Florus say no person approach to plane till he come.'

'He's on his way. I have to check the freight,' Hood said and then realized there was a strong animal smell in the cabin. The passenger compartment behind the two seats was jammed with big crates, two of them with open slatted tops bound with wire mesh. Hood bent over, peering into one of them, a small black hand grabbed his finger on the mesh and he was looking down at a little black-chinned monkey.

Monkeys . . . ? He climbed up and looked into two other open crates; more monkeys. Then, as he jumped down there were voices outside and through the open door he saw Florus waddling across from the green Citroën with Novak swaying drunkenly between Matza and one of the overalled men. Hood got out.

'Why didn't you wait for us, Conroy?' Florus said.

'I have to see the payload, don't I?'

'That is no reason.'

'I'm flying the plane. Anyway, the cargo's got to be cleared.'

'No business of yours. It is cleared already.' Florus's large, watery, grey eyes rested on Hood. He touched Hood's arm with his cane, moving him aside, and heaved himself up the steps into the passenger cabin. Matza followed with Novak and Hood stood outside watching

Florus talking quietly to Matza, giving him a rough time. Novak had slumped into one of the seats. Then Florus got out. He paused, looking at Hood, his eyes pouched up into walnuts of flesh then he snarled, 'Take off!'

Hood walked past him and climbed in.

They had to wait twenty minutes alongside the runway for an incoming Air France flight. Finally, when they were in the air and over the sea on course, Hood put the plane on automatic, lit a cigarette and looked back into the cabin. Novak was flopped back in the seat, mouth gaping. He had evidently made a heavy night of it. Matza was gloomily hunched up, chin in hand, obviously not relishing their reception on arrival.

Hood reached down, uncapped the ice-flask and poured a drink of cold orange-juice.

By the time they sighted the island, Novak had woken up and was arguing loudly with Matza. Hood took the plane down the middle of the runway, pulled up and turned and taxied to the hangar. Clayton came over with Paley, Stainburn and the other men. Switching off, Hood leant out to watch.

The cabin door opened, Novak came down the steps a little unsteadily, swayed in the sunlight and started to walk away. Clayton stepped into his path, stood glaring at him with his jaw out, suddenly threw a smash at Novak's face. Novak half blocked it with his shoulder, his head went back but he managed to keep his balance. He spat on the ground, wiped his mouth backhand and slunk off, then Matza had grabbed Clayton's arm, turning him aside, talking fast. They both threw a glance over their shoulders at Hood.

Here we go, Hood thought.

Grip in hand, he climbed down. As he was walking over to the hangar, Clayton called out, 'Hey, Conroy – just a minute. C'm here.'

DEATH IN THE ARENA

10

HOOD STOPPED. He turned and walked over to where Clayton was standing. Clayton had Matza just behind him. Beyond, round the plane, the other men had seen Clayton hit Novak and paused, looking on.

The sun came down vertically from the blue-white sky. The palm tops swayed in the breeze and made their brittle skittering sound. The light was clear and everything seemed to stand out with great distinctness. When Hood thought about the moment afterwards he always remembered this clear way everything had looked and how they had all stood still, watching. And the sense of impending violence seemed to sum up the whole feeling he had about the island – though he had no doubt that the others were all feeling it too. It was strange and powerful and Hood never quite lost it when he saw that combination of bright glare and open space and a group of still figures, their shadows short behind them, facing each other.

Clayton said, 'I hear you been getting smart, Conroy.'

'Yes?'

'I tell you to watch your step?'

'Do you expect me to wet-nurse Novak?'

'You answer me back, you big slob?'

'If you don't want the answers, don't ask the questions.'

For a second, Clayton's eyes narrowed. He stood there, poised, balanced, powerful. Then everything happened very fast. Clayton's arm shot out and grabbed Hood by the shirt collar, Hood swayed back, the heel of his hand connected hard with Clayton's chin. Clayton went backwards and fell over on his seat. For three seconds he sat there in the dust, then he made a quick movement and was up and Hood saw the razor flash in the sun.

[85

Hood dropped the bag from his left hand. Clayton crouched, head down, razor arm held away from his body. Hood waited for his rush. Somewhere beyond, a car horn was blasting persistently and impatiently and several of the men calling out, 'Mr Clayton . . . Mst' Clayton, suh . . .'

Hood watched Clayton. Suddenly Matza stepped up and grabbed Clayton's arm from behind. Clayton whirled on him, the razor coming up – then the shouts penetrated his fury and he saw the car. It was Morell in the Chrysler. Irritatedly Morell gave another long blast on the horn. Clayton's jaw was clenched. He threw a blazing look at Hood, snapped the razor away and walked quickly towards the car.

Hood watched him go, said a silent, 'Whew!' picked up the bag and headed for the lane to his hut. He could see Clayton standing talking to Morell. Then Clayton went round the bonnet and got in beside him and to Hood it seemed there was a swish of fury in the way Morell zipped the big car away down the road out of sight. Hood walked back to the hut. Inside, he lit a cigarette and stowed the bag away in a temporary hiding place. Now he had to move decisively. Trouble was obviously on the way – and yet he knew so very little more than he had when he had first reached the island.

He stood on the veranda smoking the cigarette and looking out on to the Rousseau jungle greenery. It was hard to tell how much time he had left. It could be a few hours, it could be days. Florus had obviously reported and now Clayton and Morell were deciding what they were going to do. Maybe they would be after him at once. But there was also a chance that they would do nothing until he had served his purpose – had flown in some more cargoes. It was a slim chance but this was what he had to play on. The thing was to go on as if he didn't see the risk.

He showered and changed, took the gun out and put

it inside his shirt, then went down to the base area. He praised the Lord for the early start – it was still only 10.30. As usual they had already refuelled the plane and were loading the last of the crates into a truck. He couldn't see Clayton or Novak.

Hood walked casually along to the hangar, drifted in. Stainburn was hanging about outside. At the far end, Hood stood inspecting the de Havilland, chose his moment then ducked quickly through the end door. At the last second he saw Stainburn swing as if he had seen him.

Outside he cast round. Not a vehicle in sight. He cursed, then saw Paley's little Honda motorbike parked in the shade beyond. He raced to it, shoved the bike off its stand and kicked it to life, and next minute was bumping down the slope. He didn't look back.

Even with the breeze in his face, the sun was hot. He wanted to twist the Honda up to top speed but dared not because of the blare it would make and he grit his teeth hoping that Stainburn wasn't following in a jeep. The road up the hillside was empty. At the old zoo cages he swung in, cut the engine and free-wheeled silently down the grassgrown paths between the empty pens and arenas.

He pulled up at a side path, looking back and listening. A distant sound from the road . . . then it faded. Nothing more. He started the bike again and went gently forward on low throttle until he was deep among the deserted enclosures, then pulled up and switched off.

He stood looking round – there must be a way to the big house from here. The zoo area adjoined the park round the house and the owners had surely had some easy access. He had noticed an old avenue of mahogany trees on the far side of the house when he had explored before and had reckoned they must lead down to the zoo wall.

He began to search, trying to distinguish the general lay-out of the place. Sometimes he had to leave the Honda behind and go back for it. He passed the broken and rusted cages of a monkey-house with a half-defaced enamelled sign *Macaca syl*, then a bear-pit. This part of the zoo had been designed with love and care, though now it looked hideous – rocky arches and choked grottoes, damp nooks with broken benches which must once have been pleasant shady spots. Many of the enclosures had been broken down and it was difficult to see when he was inside an old arena or out.

Going under one of the arches he found himself on a tongue of barren ground. He walked out on it a little way then as he turned back to where he had left the Honda a few yards behind, something hit his shoulder. Hood swung round.

Novak was standing thirty feet away. He still looked a little drunk, his shirt gaped open and he had the long whip in his hand. He started to laugh and as Hood faced him, the long heavy whiplash streaked out and whistled through Hood's hair. Hood ducked, pulled the gun out of his shirt – the lash hit his hand and sent the gun flying.

Hood cast round. There was no cover. He turned and ran for the arched exit in the rock, Novak moved quickly to one side, flipped the lash and Hood tripped and fell full length. Painfully he lifted himself, shook his head; small stones had bitten into his hands. Beyond, he saw Novak throwing the whiplash – once – twice – and the iron grille over the arch fell shut.

Squatting, Hood searched round for the gun. He couldn't see it. He snatched up two hunks of rock, jumped up and threw them hard at Novak. Novak side-stepped and before Hood could retreat cut him on the neck with a blow that spun him round. Grimly, Hood hunched his shoulders and ran at Novak.

Novak stood there with the whip at his side – and Hood pulled up. There was a broad concrete ditch between him and Novak; and now, glancing round, Hood saw he was in an arena, a lion's den. The rocky tongue on which he stood was surrounded on three sides by a ditch and shut off at the back by the rock wall. Novak must have followed him, watched for his opportunity and caught him here – the perfect trap. And Hood had no doubt that Novak was going to kill him. He was going to kill him at leisure.

Novak was wiping the sweat off his face with his forearm. Desperately Hood scanned the rock wall behind. Shrubs and grass grew out of it but Novak would never give him a chance to climb up. Wherever he ran, Novak could follow on the other side of the ditch and reach him. Hood remembered Belgeorge's zoo and the explanation about not giving an animal enough space to retreat for a jump. The tongue he was trapped on was designed on the same principle – too narrow between the ditches to get up a run and, near the end, a low rocky outcrop which would break a run lengthwise.

'Dance, you bastard!' Novak yelled and Hood flung himself aside, feeling the lash at his calf. He ran for the back wall, then saw the Honda against the grass covering the lower rock. It was inside! He had propped it inside the arch! As Novak lashed out again, Hood swerved. He reached the bike, kicked the starter but before he could move it, Novak's whip struck him heavily across the shoulders and neck and he tipped over with the Honda on top of him. The whip had hit a nerve in his neck and in a strange faint tingling of a thousand needles, he felt his body go numb and consciousness drifting away . . . He fought to move, dimly hearing the Honda engine still turning over. The whip bit into his leg.

Hood managed to push the bike up, raise himself. The whip clanged on the fuel tank. Then Hood was straddling the bike again and as he kicked into gear and leapt forward, the whiplash smashed over his back, making him gasp with pain.

At the end of the arena, he could hardly see, skidding round kicking up the dust. The lash missed! Novak shifted position and smashed again – Hood ducked his head behind the tank and the lash went over. Veering to miss the end wall, Hood ran on to the brink of the ditch and only just pulled round. He throttled down. If he could only keep moving he would be a little harder to hit . . . but how long could he keep it up?

His eyes were going from Novak to the ground ahead of him. He saw Novak brace, his arm begin to move. Violently he swerved, ducking his head and felt the lash catch the spokes of the front wheel. The bike checked momentarily, there was a clang and they jerked forward again. Hood looked back; the tip of the lash was on the ground. Novak had pulled the whip back and was examining it. But it would make hardly any difference.

Hood turned the bike and backed up against the rear wall and abruptly saw there was one thing he could do. The rocky outcrop which checked a lengthwise run-up extended to the ditch on either side; but on the side where Novak stood, it was a rounded hump. It would break an animal's run, but . . . Hood saw that if *he* misjudged, it was going to break his neck.

He took off, slashed through the gears and roared the engine full on. Novak stepped forward. Crouched on the bike like a mad racer, Hood went straight for the hump and the ditch. His lips came back from his teeth. Novak threw a smash, wrenched Hood's left arm off the handlebar, for a moment the Honda wobbled, tore free, then the front wheel hit the bump, lifted, Hood heaved the handlebars upward, the bike was in the air, soaring over the ditch. Hood's mouth was stretched taut.

The wheels hit the far edge of the ditch with a fearful crunch. Hood thought he was going over the front, gripped madly with his knees and hung on and next second was on balance flying forward and skidding the bike round. Over!

Hood roared the engine head-on for Novak. Novak raised the whip and as the bike reached him, it hit another bump. At full throttle the Honda reared up and smashed into Novak's chest. The impact lifted Novak clear off the ground and threw him fifteen feet. Hood took the shock, the machine went sideways and as it landed, he sprawled over with it, wrenching himself madly away to stop the up-ended handlebar getting him in the groin.

He picked himself up. Novak was on his back, one leg twitching. Hood limped over. Novak's head was on the stone edge of the ditch, a dark stain forming under it. As Hood stood panting, looking down at him, Novak stopped moving. Hood took hold of his feet, dragged him round and tipped him into the ditch. The body fell into the weeds and, leaning over, Hood could only see Novak's legs.

He straightened up, sweating and shaking, feeling all the welts of the whip at once. His hand came away from his neck bloody. He lifted the Honda on the stand and looked into the mirror. The weals on his neck were pretty ugly. His leg hurt like hell and he had to try three times to light a cigarette, holding one hand with the other.

He sat down, dabbing his neck and gingerly fingering the other lash marks. Morell and Co. would obviously soon find that Novak was missing. Well, it had been one or other of them.

After a while he began to feel better. The tremor had gone, though he was very thirsty. He got to his feet, started up the Honda and rode slowly back to the entrance of the lion's arena, heaved up the grille and found the gun.

Then he rode slowly along the path getting his bearings. Almost at once he found what he had been looking for – a broad main path leading up to an iron gate in the wall through which he could see the avenue of trees to the house.

He hid the Honda in the high weeds and walked to the gate. A gap at the side had been closed with barbed wire. The wire sagged under his foot and he ducked through. Keeping to the grass, he went up to the house; the high door at the end of the avenue looked as if it had been bolted for half a century and the windows were shuttered. He turned the angle of the house and caught a faint smell of cooking — kitchen quarters? A door ahead was open. He could hear nothing and put his head in; it was an old-fashioned stone-floored kitchen with huge sinks, pots boiling on the range, a door on the far side. Whoever was cooking had just stepped out.

Hood went swiftly through the far door into a big service pantry cluttered with wrecks of chairs and rusted utensils. A narrow boxed-in stair led up. He sprang up, pushed the door at the top and was in a dingy passage with rooms on either side, the old servants' accommodation. He followed this round and at the end stepped through into a hallway.

A splash of sunlight through some hole lit up the place and Hood stared — cracked and mildewed portraits hung on the walls or lay where they had fallen, great mahogany chairs and chests stood thick with cobwebs, plaster had dropped from the ceiling showing the laths. Everything smelled of dust and death.

Somewhere beyond a door slammed, echoing. Hood halted, listening, then ducked behind a tall-backed chair. In a minute the big turbaned negress he had seen before stomped past. As the passage door clacked behind her, Hood stepped out and ran tiptoe along the hall. At the end was a gallery with doors right and left. The first was jammed, he pushed the second and at first made out only the bright bars of sunlight through the half-open shutters, then saw the big brass bedstead and on the far side of it

Kim McCaine looking at him with a frightened face.

She had nothing on and Hood's heart began bumping, seeing her full breasts, their firm heaviness swaying as she moved, her small waist and pouting hairless little pouch, the long tapering thighs. She had one hand lifted to her face, was biting her lip but not trying to hide herself and he pushed the door wide, then caught the shift of her eyes and swung round. The negro he had seen before was behind the door.

He was a small hard-looking man and his eyes were steady. He obviously knew what Hood had come for. Facing him, Hood shoved the door shut behind him. The man edged warily away, Hood gestured to the girl to skirt round the other side of the room to the door. She moved out of his sight and said, 'There's a woman . . .'

There was a fractional pause. He heard the window rattle, glanced over quickly, seeing her trying to pull it shut and the negro lunged. Hood caught the flash of something lifted, snapped double, arm raised to block the forearm and as the man's weight came on him, he shot violently upright, pitching him over his shoulder.

The man went across the room and hit the wall with a thick smack head-first. He lay on his face, made a feeble gesture then was still.

Kim McCaine was backed to the window, biting her lip. 'The woman's below . . . I thought he'd call out.' Hood stepped over, looked down at the man – he wasn't going to move again.

'Kim—' She ran to him and pressed herself into his arms, her breasts warm against the opening of his shirt. He felt himself stirring, lifted her face and kissed her on the lips and quickly kissed her shoulders and breasts. 'Where are your clothes?'

'They've taken them away.'

He put her away, in two strides was at the bed, yanked a sheet off it and with a heave tore off a broad strip. 'Come here, quick.' He took her nude waist, held the sheet against her. 'Turn – pivot.' She did so and he tucked the end of the sheet into the top. It made a little miniskirt and looking at her in it, he couldn't help feeling a jolt. He pulled off his shirt, popping the buttons, threw it at her while he went to the door and checked outside. Nobody. When he turned back she was at his elbow.

'Do you know a way out not through the kitchen?'

She nodded. Outside, she led down the main stairs to the ground floor. In the far room was a broken window with the shutter fixed inside. The shutter screeched as he forced it wide, they jumped out on to the terrace. Hood made her duck behind the stone balustrade and then they broke clear and ran. She was out of breath when they dropped in the grass half-way down the slope to the zoo wall. He stuck his head up, scanning the house, the hill-side and the surrounding trees. No sign of the guards yet.

'Where are we going?' she said. The buttons had gone from the shirt and she was leaning back with her breasts showing, a film of perspiration shining on them, and he thought she was very pretty.

'I don't know. Clear from here first.'

'What are those marks on your neck?'

He had forgotten them. 'Long story. Can you run some more?'

She nodded. They ran panting down to the zoo gate, got through and she climbed on to the Honda pillion. Hood steered them bumping down the zoo paths to the entrance gates – and there was only one way to turn, towards the base. The other way simply led back to the plantation house.

Hood said, 'Hold tight, we've got to freewheel.' He felt her as she pressed herself closely against him, her legs gripping him and her arms coming farther round him as he swung down the road. There was a track to the beach below if he could find it.

They swerved round the curves and as the slope began to level out, he saw the track ahead. They turned in and ten minutes later were within sight of the sea. At the top of the beach, Hood found a half-collapsed shelter of palm branches, hid the Honda and led her in.

It was cool in the shade. She touched his neck gently. 'But you're hurt.'

'It's all right.'

'How did you get here? Why—?'

'Kim, listen,' he took her hands. 'They're going to be after us. Tell me one thing – do you know what they're doing here, what it means, Varuna Reef, the base camp, all this?'

Her eyes were scared in the semi-gloom. 'Don't you know?'

'Looking for oil?' He didn't believe it.

'No.'

'Then what? What's that stuff in the huts, the machinery? What does it do?'

She looked away. 'If you don't know – I . . .'

'Come on, what is it? We're on our own and I need to know.'

There was a pause. 'There are a group of men. They are going to do something awful.'

'What?'

'I only know some of it.'

He looked at her, seeing the effort she was making to keep her nerve. The mole over her eyebrow made her look beautifully touching and a trickle of sweat ran down her neck over the rich swell of her right breast. Her hand touched his and Hood said, 'It's all right, don't be afraid.'

'Promise we'll get away.'

He knew he couldn't promise but he said, 'Of course. They're not going to hurt you. Here—' He held out his cigarettes and she took one and he lit them both. 'Tell me what you know.'

[95

'I came here with Morell. We went to New York that evening, the evening of the London party and came on here. The machines in the huts are extractors.'

'What for?'

'They're used in cosmetics – making scent. You put dried flowers in, the extractor grinds them to powder, washes them over in a light solvent and extracts the essential oils. This gives you the basis for scent.'

'Scent?' It sounded absurd . . . wildly incongruous, then he remembered the maker's plate and the mark on the machines, the cyrillic Ж. 'What was that mark—?'

'Princess Zherkov.'

'Of course, Princess Zherkov! A make of cosmetics, wasn't it?'

She nodded. 'I worked for them. The Ж was the trademark – lipstick, facepowder, scent, what they used to call *fards* – so old-fashioned but so nice.'

Now Hood remembered – the Princess Zherkov things had been famous, the chic and glamour of another age, used by all the great in the Diaghileff days, now clung to only by ancient dames and faded actresses; they had never changed and he supposed, like others, he had unconsciously marvelled at the firm's continued existence.

She said, 'They were gradually dying, going broke, everybody was very old and marvellous; there really was a Princess Zherkov, I loved them all. I was working with them in Grasse, learning. Then one day Morell came and he seemed to have control. He took me to London, kept close after me, I hardly knew anybody – and, well, he was rich and attentive. I did very little work in London . . . we seemed to be waiting. Nothing in the firm changed and it seemed a little strange. I heard they had begun dismantling one or two extractors at Grasse but I didn't know they had been sent here until Morell brought me here from New York.'

'But Kim,' he leaned forward speaking urgently. 'It

simply doesn't account for things. Why in God should they want extractors here? They're not making scent or face-cream. This isn't — this isn't just some commercial enterprise. It's another dimension.'

She stubbed out her cigarette. 'You use the same extractors for insecticides.'

'Insecticides?' Somehow it was strange and menacing and yet all the incongruity vanished at once. He saw this was the secret — or was close to it — she had understood it and Morell had known he couldn't let her get away, if ever he had intended her to.

'Some of the scent firms hire out their extractors in the off-season to insecticide-makers. We used to.' Hood stared at her in silence. She said, 'I think they are going to make something much worse, I don't know what, but something horrible.'

He stared across at the green-yellow glare beyond the shelter. 'Flowers . . . They're growing flowers on the slope of the mountain on the north side here, fields of them, you can see them from the air.'

'Pyrethrum flowers.'

'Yes?' He looked at her quickly. What had he learned about pyrethrum flowers? He turned away, dragged on the cigarette, racking his brains to think, then swung back. 'But do you mean they bought up Princess Zherkov just to get hold of the extractors? Surely they'd—'

'No, no. The firm's still going; they are using it as a screen. Don't you see? I tried to go back to Grasse but Morell stopped me. They have done it very carefully and very cleverly, without making a stir. Nobody has noticed.'

'You mean they're operating behind Princess Zherkov, using the plant and so forth as if they were making the old cosmetics?'

'Yes.'

It was the perfect camouflage, of course, if you were making something secretly. Who would investigate anything so rundown and faded and obsolete – especially when there had been no outward change?

She said, 'I believe they are going to transfer here when the time comes . . . that's one of the reasons for Varuna Reef.'

'But meantime they're running it from Grasse?'

'No. There's a place in Touraine called Les Gerfauts. I've heard Morell talk about it. I think that's their centre.'

'Did Morell tell you why he came here specifically?'

'No. I didn't know we were coming here at all. We were supposed to be going to New York, then it was Nassau. Then we went to Guadaloupe and came on in the yacht. When I wanted to get out, he kept me in that house. He was furious I got out that day when you saw me. He's impotent and he's pathological about it.'

'I see . . .'

'He used to tie me down on the bed . . . try to get himself worked up . . . it took ages . . . and in the end, sometimes, he'd finally do it—' She looked away.

Hood put his arm round her and smoothed her hair. 'It's all right now.'

He left her and went to the door. There was nobody in sight. Through the palm trunks he could see the yacht offshore. He stood looking out, thinking of what to do then turned back. 'Listen, Kim, I've got to leave you. I want you to stay here till I get back. All right?'

She looked at him pleadingly. 'How long?'

'Not long. Keep a lookout; if you see anybody coming, you'd better get into the bushes, lie down but don't go away, I want to find you here when I get back.'

'Can't I come with you?'

He took her shoulders, she was looking up at him with a little perspiration on her upper lip and then her cool mouth was on his and her arms holding him. In a moment she broke away and turned her head, a little short of breath and her hand crushed his hard and tight. The shirt hung open and he looked at her, desiring her. He took her chin, made her look at him.

'Keep your nerve, kid.'

She nodded silently, her eyes on his.

'We're going to be dead by tonight if we don't, both of us.' He pulled the gun out, checked that it was off safety and gave it to her. 'Don't use it unless you have to.'

'I'll be here.'

He pulled her to him and held her in a long kiss, his hands going over her bare back, then he stepped outside and went quickly towards the air base.

A SLIM CHANCE

I I

GETTING THROUGH the undergrowth made a lot of noise and he paused every hundred yards listening. At the base the sun fell vertically on the deserted open space; they were all evidently at the mess. Everything was silent.

On the far side was a solitary figure, the fuel truck driver, walking across to one of the huts; and then, as Hood watched, Paley came out of the hangar wiping his hands on cotton waste. Paley? Working on the aircraft? Hood groaned inwardly. *Was the aircraft out of commission?*

Quickly he shifted position. The Commander was standing half out of the hangar with the door open and part of the starboard turbo engine cowling off. What was he to do? It was urgent to take advantage of this lull – it couldn't last much longer. The woman in the house would find Kim gone and then the balloon was going up. Bring Kim to the aircraft now? He felt in desperate doubt. No – go on. He grit his teeth, plunged through the tangled greenery and in a few minutes could see the back of his bungalow. He edged nearer. Two of Clayton's men were lounging under a tree on the other side of the lane, obviously posted to report his return.

Keeping the bungalow between them, Hood ran across and ducked among the weeds and piles under the veranda. He fished out the package of plastic and time pencils, blessing Ernesto, broke the plastic into two lumps and stuffed one into each trousers pocket. He pushed the pencils down alongside and turned back. To keep under cover, he had to go round the hangar again and at the beach, went forward through the low scrub beyond the seaward end of the runway towards Varuna Reef.

He could see no movement along the tarmac road.

The edges of the sunblinds outside the clubhouse flapped gently. The intermittent flash of glass came from one of the powerboats moving at the jetty. The quiet emptiness of everything somehow seemed ominous.

Hood ran across the tarmac road into the shrubbery and turned towards the main clubhouse building – then snapped to a halt. Ahead in the trees was a wooden pylon with a ladder to a platform above. The platform was high among the palmheads and looking up Hood could see it carried guns. A gun tower! One gun looked like a Bofors, the other a heavy machine-gun. Behind them was a little palmbranch shelter and as he stared, Hood caught a movement – the guns were manned.

He said quietly, God Almighty. The tower was so well concealed that he had not glimpsed it from the plane. Now, he could see there was an arc of fire through the trees to seaward; but the guns were obviously meant chiefly against aircraft. How many more guns did they have in the place? The beaches were probably covered too.

Kneeling under cover, he took out the plastic. He tore off a hunk – it was like stiff plasticine – and moulded it in his hands into the shape of a hollow melon with a hole at one end. It made his hands shake. Then he took out the time pencils; they were transparent tubes like cheap ballpoints. He chose one stamped 20, crunched it hard with his teeth, breaking down the tiny division separating the acids inside, and dug it into the plastic melon. In twenty minutes the united acids in the pencil would detonate and explode the plastic.

He stuffed the rest back into his shirt and crept forward with the bomb. As he reached among the foliage round the legs, his shirt caught on concealed barbed wire and some tins attached banged faintly. He crouched motionless, cursing.

Carefully he worked himself free, reached in and lobbed the bomb inside. It vanished into the grass and for a minute Hood crouched there staring baffled and helpless, then tore himself away. It would have to do – he couldn't spare the time.

He ran on to the clubhouse. Through the open side facing him he could see two servants in white inside serving somebody at a table. Morell? A screen blocked the view. Hood ducked down, made a thirty-minute plastic bomb and tiptoed in. A man stepped out from behind a pillar in front of him, back turned.

Hood froze. Soundlessly he bent down, pushed the bomb behind an armchair and backed away. The open grass to the bushes outside seemed a mile wide and as he reached cover he saw the man turn, as if he had spotted him.

Hood ran crouching towards the jetty. One last thing – try to knock the boats out. Then as he flattened in the scrub, scanning beach and jetty, a low moan like the sound of some neanderthal animal came out of the trees behind him and wound up into a rising and falling wail. A siren!

It was loud and close, a general alarm. Christ! Hood held his breath, then lifted himself. A party of men with rifles was coming towards him along the beach five hundred yards away.

Moving back into cover, Hood belted for the air base. At the runway, he dropped flat, getting his breath, looking out over the open spaces. Somebody hurried away round the corner of the hangar but that was all so far.

Hood reached the far side and tore through the undergrowth. The siren was still going and the parrots in the trees were screaming. As he came in sight of the shelter, his breath rasping, Kim ran out of the bushes.

'What is it?' She looked very scared and held on to him.

'It's for us. Give me the gun. Come on.'

Gripping her hand, he forced her along fast. Presently she pulled him up, gasping. Above the wail they heard voices and movement through the vegetation close behind.

Hood grabbed her, pressed back against a tree and they saw another patrol of about eight men go by towards the beach. Now they were between two patrols.

The sound of a truck came from beyond. They would soon have the dogs out from the camouflaged area. The whole place was in action. They ran on through the thick leaves and vines. Now the siren had moaned to a stop and every movement they made seemed alarmingly loud. Presently the back of the hangar loomed through the trees ahead. Breathless, they crept up and looked through the leaves.

The red fuel tanker was parked on the open ground near the back corner of the hangar and, half hidden behind it, was a squat, camouflaged armoured scout car mounting twin machine-guns. Clayton was standing beside the scout car talking into a hand mike. It was obviously their radio control car – and the patrols were out with walkie-talkies. Five men, all with automatic rifles, were standing by, waiting for Clayton's orders.

The big sliding door of the hangar, wide open, was only fifty yards away – but it was fifty yards of open ground with Clayton and the men in between. As Hood watched, Clayton dropped the mike and turned to the men. He pointed in Hood's direction, then swung in a narrow arc to the beach, assigning them a sector. The men only had to walk straight across to find them.

Hood lifted the gun. Kill Clayton first – but even if he got three or four of the others, it would still leave the gunner on the scout car. A plastic bomb? He could use a short pencil, hold it till the last seconds and then toss it like a hand grenade – he'd seen it done in Algeria. They would have to rush the hangar, hoping to make it in the confusion. He grit his teeth – Christ, it was a slim chance. The fuel tanker, loaded with high octane, was close by and if it went up too it was going to be curtains for everybody. Yet it looked like their only hope.

It meant closing the range. There was a tall screen of vegetation at the limit of their cover about twenty yards along to Hood's right – as close as he could get to the scout car.

Hood wiped the sweat off his face. In a scared voice Kim whispered, 'Darling, can't we try the beach?'

'No good.' Hood stuck the gun into his belt, jerked his head to her to follow and moved right. He had the plastic in his hands, kneading it into a rough ball. In his pocket he felt three pencils. He snatched his eyes away from the men to look at them – all three-minute pencils. Yet had they got even three minutes more? He bit one, held it in his hand, mentally counting. Clayton, his back turned, was answering somebody on the radio. The five men were waiting for his word to go.

Then Terry Windmiller came round the far side of the scout car into the open. She was hatless, in a brown silk suit, and even at that moment Hood couldn't help thinking she was cool and lovely. She had obviously been there all the time and she stood watching Clayton. Hood wanted to yell at her to go away! Suddenly, close at his back, Kim let out a stifled scream.

'Ants . . . We're in an ants' nest!' She was upright.

Hood made a wild grab for her, saw Terry Windmiller snap a look straight at them, then he had pulled Kim down under cover again, feeling the ants now swarming over his own legs. The crawling mass were coming out of the grass, big black ants, biting ferociously.

The two of them crouched, stamping and trying to kick the ants off. The ants ran up their legs, it was excruciating – a thousand bites a second. In agony, Hood flung the time pencil away across the bushes and beat at the black swarm on Kim's legs. Clayton barked an order and Hood heard the men start across. This was it. He turned, pulled the gun.

The steps crunched over towards them, suddenly

stopped yards away and now Hood could hear Terry arguing with Clayton. She was holding up the men, trying to give him a chance to get away with Kim – and at that moment there was a sound like a muffled shot from beyond. The time pencil!

Clayton and the men snapped round, staring away in this new direction, then they all charged over in a body. Clayton was shouting orders. Hood could hear them in the undergrowth away to the right.

'Now – run!' It was Terry's voice, soft and urgent. Hood blessed her, grabbed Kim's arm, they broke cover and raced for the hangar. As they swung inside, Hood tugged the last chunk of plastic out of his pocket, bit a pencil and stuck it in. He slung it under the de Havilland and ran like mad for the Commander ahead. Kim slammed the door behind him and he jumped for the controls.

Was the plane going to start? As he made the contact there was a blast from the trees ahead – the gun tower bomb. The port engine roared into life. Hood's mouth was strained taut – then the starboard engine was on. He yelled, 'Hold on!' and they were rolling clear of the hangar and swinging out across the runway.

Behind him, Kim yelled, 'They're coming back – getting into the car.' He revved the engines and they bumped fast up the broad empty stretch of the runway towards the distant trees. The runway ended at the beach, so that he was going to have to run back inland, turn for the take-off and go past them. Suddenly through the roar he caught the heavy slam of machine-gun fire. The scout car was shooting. Hood saw a line spit up just ahead across the runway, veered madly. As he swerved back, a crack came from astern – they were hit. Then from the hangar there was an explosion, an igniting flash and a great rolling roar.

'The fuel truck!'

[105

Hood craned round. The hangar bomb had gone up, blown the de Havilland fuel and the tanker as well. Black billows with fiery insides were curling over the hangar area and several fires had started in the trees. He could see one of the beach patrols running in. As he strained forward watching the runway and the control panel he had a long stab of agony – what had happened to Terry? He prayed she hadn't been hurt.

He swung the plane, gave it the gun and roared down the runway. The plane gathered speed. Smoke was drifting across, he saw two men on the Varuna Reef side lift guns and had the impression bullets had hit, then he eased the stick back, she lifted and they were airborne. He hoped to God there were no more gun towers.

Suddenly to starboard there was a flash and the clubhouse bomb sent up a shower of glass and debris. They sailed through the smoke. He couldn't see any of the Clayton group. Now the beach was below and the sea. He kept low over the water, steering for the yacht to discourage any fire from the shore, sheered off at the last minute and began to climb. He could see them staring up on deck.

Kim came up behind him. 'My God . . . I never thought we'd do it.' She had found a suit of white overalls and steadied herself to climb into it.

Hood said, 'I think they've hit us somewhere. The plane's acting up. I don't know how far we can get.' Maybe it was Paley's uncompleted repair, he thought; but he didn't tell her that.

ON THE OTHER SIDE

<table>
<tr><td>12</td></tr>
</table>

OVER GRENADA the first thing they saw was a cricket match. Kim shouted, 'If you want to know something, that's the first game of cricket I've really loved seeing.'

Hood shrugged – he had the head-set on, listening to the St George's control tower. The starboard engine was missing badly and he thought it was going to pack up. They circled over the postcard harbour of St George's, Hood lined up and put the plane down. Unexpectedly the engine held out and minutes later they were taxiing to the airport building.

In the neat white-painted immigration hall, Hood rang Rathborne, the local Banner Oil man and by the time they had gone through the explanations about having no papers to a junior then a senior officer – who stared stonily at their odd costumes – Rathborne was sailing in through the doors, a plump smiling man.

Rathborne had mighty pull and push. In thirty minutes they were through and sitting with drinks on Rathborne's veranda overlooking the harbour. An hour later, he had arranged for new passports and Hood had dictated a long telex to Lovatt in London reporting the main events. The message ended, 'Now consider it urgent locate operating centre in France before Morell group can dismantle or cover tracks. Am proceeding Orly forthwith. Regards Hood.'

At six o'clock when Hood and Kim came back from a quick trip to buy clothes, they found that Rathborne had laid on a charter flight to Barbados and onward passage by Panam via Miami.

Rathborne said, 'Be quicker through Guadaloupe, actually. You sure you don't want to——?'

'Well, we don't love Miami, who could, but we have

[107

some friends on the lookout at Pointe-à-Pitre and we'd rather give them a miss.'

Rathborne nodded.

'Burn that telex tape, John, will you?'

'Right away.'

'And keep the lid on this whole thing – tight.'

'I will.'

*

'*Nous venons d'atterrir à Orly. Il est 9 heures 35, heure locale, et la température au sol est de 19 degrés . . .*' The hostess's voice came over the intercom. Beside Hood, Kim stifled a yawn. The flight from Washington had been half empty and Hood had woken from the intermittent snatches of sleep and seen her sitting silent and wakeful with the light still on over her seat. He had tried to get her to say what was the matter.

'I suppose I'm still scared of Morell.'

'But not here, sweetheart? We're away from them.'

'You don't know these people.'

Upstairs they filed out into the long departure hall. The place was crowded. Streams of people drifted back and forth, rows stood staring at the departures board. Kim said, 'I must go and wash and clean up. Wait for me.'

'All right.' He walked along with her past the escalators to the end of the hall, watched her go ahead then followed himself and turned into the men's. As he came out again, the woman attendant bobbed up over her saucer and gave him a flinty glare.

Idly Hood wandered round the showcases of scent, dolls, apostle spoons, gigantic boxes of chocolates, monstrous toys. A troop of Japanese went by, always so neat and pleased. He turned, watching the entrance for Kim, turned back again, strolled to the window, drifted round the showcases again. Chimes kept sounding as the Americanized voice announced departures and arrivals, '. . . gate numberr thirdy-seven . . .'

He turned again. Where was she? He had been waiting too long. Panic gripped him. Hold it . . . hold it . . . this is Orly and it's morning. Quickly he strode across. 'Have you seen a girl in a blue and white dress, a blonde, short hair?'

The woman, a hard-faced fifty in white starched apron, stared at him dumb and Hood stepped past her into the tiled halls of the women's section.

'A gauche, monsieur!'

He kept going.

'Mais . . .!'

In six paces, Hood was inside and scanning the wash-basin area. Two women at the glass turned and stared back, a bolt shot and a girl came out of a cubicle flicking at her skirt which was caught up; she stared too. Hood called out, 'Kim.' No answer. She wasn't there. Hood turned and strode for the exit.

'Mais, monsieur!'

How was it possible? How could she have missed him—she'd been too nervous to wander away on her own. Had she come out and thought he'd gone? Hurrying, he weaved in and out of the crush. *They had got her.*

'Mais, monsieur! Monsieur . . .!'

He couldn't see her. He pushed through the ranks at the departures board. Heads were turning at him.

'Mais . . . stop that man . . . arrêtez cet homme! . . . Arretêz-le . . .'

Suddenly he was aware of the woman – the toilet attendant was chasing him. There was a swirl in the crowd and he saw two burly blue-suited men like airport cops making for him. Visions of charges rose up . . . *attentat à la pudeur* . . . He suppressed a desire to run, turned round and the next minute the men had grabbed him and the toilet woman was pushing and panting up.

'Look,' Hood began impatiently, 'I was—'

'Cet homme . . .' She gasped for breath.

'What's he done?' one of the men said. 'Le salaud.'

'Salopard!'

'C'était une saloperie, mémère?'

'Mais la soucoupe, monsieur. La soucoupe!'

'What?' Then Hood understood. She was outraged all right – he hadn't paid. Gummily she was explaining to the men.

'Il entre deux fois, hommes et femmes, il passe devant, mais *il paie pas*! Une fois peut-être, deux fois non! non! non!'

Hood dug in his pocket, fished out two francs.

'La soucoupe, hein? C'est mon manger, hein?' She was stretching her neck at him. 'Comment je fais avec la petite Danielle sans la soucoupe, hein?'

He wanted to shut her up, held out a five-franc note; her withered paw snatched it.

'Quand même y a des gens, hein? Ils croient qu'on vit pour rien.' Tilting their heads to one side, the men looked Hood over obliquely, moved slowly away. The old duck was waddling back, muttering to herself. Hood stood there. The whole thing was a madly incongruous phantasmagoria – as if, in some strange way, life had suddenly jolted into a wrong groove, exactly as it had seemed, he remembered, on the island.

He searched through the hall again, went downstairs – Kim had gone. Now he was sure Morell's men had picked her up and had seen him too. He was racked by self-reproach.

He went out, took a taxi into Paris and paid it off at the Hôtel St James's in the Faubourg St Honoré. He walked in past the hall porter, through the building to the rue de Rivoli. It was one of three exits – number three through the bar – and they couldn't watch them all. He stopped a cruising cab, drove to the Avis office and forty minutes later he was holding the big blue Plymouth at eighty along the N10 road to Chartres and Tours.

Tortured by thoughts of Kim he kept the car at a good speed. At Tours, he crossed the river and pulled up at a café. The Michelin map in the car showed nowhere called

Les Gerfauts, the place Kim had spoken of as Morell's headquarters – and he wondered in desperation if she had got it right. The café was clean and bright. Hood ordered a sandwich and a glass of wine and when he asked for Les Gerfauts, the man thought it was, 'Down by Montbazon.'

Hood drove across town and found a policeman. The policeman thought he had heard of it somewhere between l'Ile Bouchard and Richelieu. L'Ile Bouchard was thirty kilometres on.

Hood drove through the sunny early afternoon. The country was sumptuous in its greens and greys and browns, subtly different from the English field-browns. But the image of Kim's scared look kept coming at him in the windscreen and he trod down on the pedal. A black Peugeot 404 that had been behind for some time had gone, but now there was a blue Porsche.

A sign said Ile Bouchard, 15 kilometres. Hood swung off before the Porsche came over the rise behind and ran between high winding hedgerows for a kilometre or so then came out into the open. After another five kilometres he crossed a bridge and turned south.

He could have believed himself a hundred miles from anywhere – fields all round, a grey wall here and there, nobody moving. Small unmarked roads led off at intervals. He looked back, couldn't see the Porsche. The road narrowed and he wondered if he had missed the turning. Then at a crossing he saw a man and pulled up; a rough-looking farmer with an ancient Citroën 11 behind him.

Hood said, 'Bonjour, monsieur. Can you tell me where Les Gerfauts is?'

The man's small brown eyes went over Hood, he sucked something from a tooth. 'Down yonder.' He jerked his head.

Hand on the gear lever, Hood hesitated. There was something strange about the man and he gazed back at him for what must have been an oddly long time, then snapped out of it, said 'Thanks' and drove on.

Half a mile farther, the surface became a brown stony track. He passed signs to invisible farms: Chez Perrifard ... Chez Buffont ... driving slowly among the potholes. And abruptly it clicked in his mind that he had noticed sunglasses in the man's pocket just now. A French farmer with sunglasses?

Now the light had changed and a big black cloud was stretching over the sky, darkening the landscape and it had all quite quickly become different. Rain whipped across the windscreen; the brown earth was cold. He pulled the wheel over and out of the corner of his eye saw a black Citroën coming fast out of the farm track to his right. He trod down on the pedal. As the Plymouth leapt forward, the window glass beside him shattered, he ducked, hearing the burst of fire clanging into the bodywork behind.

For a moment he held the charging Plymouth on the road, another burst showered the windscreen. The car lurched violently, hit something – Hood couldn't see – the door burst open and he pitched headlong out on to stones and grass. The Citroën tyres drummed past his head and there was another long burst of tommy-gun fire into the crashed Plymouth.

Hood got to his knees in the ditch. The Citroën had stopped beyond and men were piling out. He heard their running steps on the road. Doubled up, Hood ran back a few yards to a hump at the roadside, then broke away behind it across the field. The heavy earth clung to his shoes. At first they didn't see him – he snatched a look back; they were still busy round the crashed car – then he heard their voices raised excitedly. They were after him.

He ran hard, the slanting rain stinging him. There was a copse on a rise ahead but he couldn't see a house anywhere. The earth became lumpier and he was running through a crop of cabbages and slowed up. Looking back, he could see the men coming after him and the Citroën at a distance moving round on his right to outflank him.

His shoes were clogged with mud, he slogged through the cabbages and forced himself into a chest-bursting spurt up the rise to reach the cover of the copse.

In among the trees, he flopped, bent over, hands on knees with his head hanging, the blood drumming in his ears and his breath rasping. In a minute he turned and ran on again – suddenly pitched forward and went sprawling full length in the leaves. Painfully he pulled his leg out of the rabbit hole and got up; his left ankle was burning like hell and when he pulled the sock down he could see it was going to swell.

He stood up, tried it, winced as it took his weight. The men were coming across the fields. He hobbled through the trees, came out on the far side. The fields ran away in rounded humps, like cushions, with folds and trees in between but hardly a hedge anywhere. On the right, some men from the Citroën were coming fast across the field, others were running towards him on his left. His ankle had ballooned.

He ran flinching down the slope, every step agony, making for the nearest fold. The men on his right shouted, seeing him, and the crack of a gun came over distantly in the still air. He was still out of range.

He tried to run faster but couldn't do it. On the fresh rise, he nearly tripped and fell but kept up. Cresting the hump of the field, he could see a tall screen of poplars and some willows in the fold below and forced himself, limping, down to them. At the bottom was a stream, he let himself down off the bank into three feet of water and waded across, stumbling and gasping, and splashed through the shallows on the far side. The trees hid him from the field behind.

In front of him was a hedge of rhododendrons, he broke through and stood looking across a formal French garden at the façade of a great eighteenth-century stone house.

Breathless, he sagged with relief, hobbled over. There

was a noble terrace, steps up, ornamental pots, a coat of arms over the studded door. Brocade curtains draped the windows. He pulled the heavy bronze bellknob. Looking back, he could see nothing of the fields behind and no movement through the trees.

The door opened and he turned round. A tall, thin, upright man faced him – iron-grey hair, grey brush moustache, wearing a brown sports coat and flannel trousers. 'Oh,' the man said in English. 'Oh—Good afternoon.'

The Englishness of him caught Hood with a shock of surprise and enormous thankfulness. A pleasant smile came into the man's face, lifting the edge of the moustache and crinkling the corners of the pale blue eyes. There was the stamp of gentle kindness and good manners on him.

'Good afternoon,' Hood said. 'I've – uh – had a little trouble with my car. I wonder if I could use your telephone?'

'But of course. Come in.'

In the great stone-flagged hall four long R.A.F. banners hung from the beams above, floating out now in the air through the open door, and there were shields on the walls between standing suits of armour, medieval chests and tall-backed chairs. Everything was very quiet.

'You are not hurt, I trust? Oh but—' He looked down at Hood's mud-caked shoes and trousers, slowly up at the shirt, wrenched-down tie, the small cuts and scratches on Hood's face. '—but you are. You are. My dear sir, you must have attention.'

'It really isn't much,' Hood said. 'I sprained my ankle; if I could get a cold bandage on that I'll be all right.'

'Yes, yes. We'll arrange that at once. Oh—' He turned back apologetically. 'My name's Peter Wynyard.'

'And mine's Charles Hood.'

'I'm happy to meet you, Mr Hood. Come along, we'll soon have you right.'

He led the way past the staircase, through a library and smaller rooms to a vast sunny stone-floored room with tall windows overlooking the gardens at the back of the house. Hood limped in and stood gazing. There were silver-laid shields all round the room, blue R.A.F. flags and standards with squadron numbers on them, four or five mounted propellers, a model Spitfire in silver, a Hurricane in bronze, clay busts of young men.

A private museum? Somehow in spite of the sun the light in the room struck cold. There were deep chairs beside the monumental fireplaces, pipes and books and newspapers lying around – it was obviously here with all this commemorative stuff that Mr Wynyard lived. Hood thought it was a little overpowering.

'Oh, you're looking at my memorial things. Come in, Mr Hood. Let me give you a whisky and soda. Steady you up – or d'you prefer brandy?'

'Whisky. Thank you.'

'Sit you down. Get off that leg.'

Choosing an upright chair, Hood glanced at Wynyard as he crossed to a cupboard and brought out decanter and glasses. There was something vaguely and distantly reminiscent. 'It's kind of you,' Hood said. 'Where were you with the R.A.F.?'

'Oh—' the gentle smile. 'All over, you know . . .'

'At home, in 1940?'

'Yes . . . yes . . .'

He was too old to have been in Spitfires – still sharp and active but decidedly too old. He must have been at some Command H.Q. 'Fighter Command, perhaps?' Hood said.

'Yes, I was. During all that.' He turned and brought the whisky over, put the heavy crystal glass on the table beside Hood's chair. Hood glanced at it – and saw that the marquetry table-top was a ouija board. He glanced up at Wynyard. Wynyard was standing there looking steadily at him. There was something a little strange, only for a few seconds, in the way Wynyard was poised there, looking at him. Wynyard had seen he had noticed the ouija board and he smiled again.

'Yes . . . Have you – anybody there, Mr Hood. On the other side?'

'No.'

The pale eyes held his, with a flicker of indulgence now, and then Wynyard turned and went back to his own glass. Hood took a drink; it struck him again how quiet the house was – and he hadn't seen a servant. Wynyard was facing him with his glass.

'There are many of them here now, you know . . . They all come here, my boys.'

'You mean pilots?'

'Yes . . . Oh and gunners too. I talk to them all . . . There are many. They are happy on the other side . . . sometimes there are bad periods—' his voice hardened, '—but I talk to them . . .'

Suddenly he began to speak as if there were somebody else in the room. 'Now it won't do . . . look here . . . I know, old chap, but . . . well, all right then, tonight . . .' He broke off, smiled. 'So sorry, Mr Hood . . . you see, some of them want to come back . . . they were so young, so young . . . they're very happy over there . . . but it's . . . it's not the same . . . They miss things . . . they're still just as they were, on the other side, they've not got old like we have . . . and sometimes it's hard to make them understand . . . that's what's so awful . . . and then there's trouble . . . But I try, do my best . . . they're all my boys.'

'What happens when there's trouble?' Hood said.

'Oh – they get rough . . . throw things . . . smash— Now, Roger . . . look here, old boy, you . . .'

The sudden crash made Hood jolt, he was on his feet wincing and lifting his bad ankle. A shield on the other side of the room had flown several feet through the air and smashed against the window-frame. Hood stared. Was it possible . . .?

He caught Wynyard's still and steady gaze on him, then Wynyard smiled again. 'I'm sorry. I apologize, Mr Hood . . . this isn't a good introduction . . . Oh – but I've been forgetting. You're hurt, my dear fellow. Your ankle . . . We must get you seen to.'

He strode alertly across the room and touched a bell by the fireplace. Hood sat down again, there was a little pause and as Hood bent over to ease off his shoe, somebody came in. Hood looked up and said, Christ! to himself.

It was a man . . . he believed it was a man . . . The head and torso were entirely swathed in white bandages that seemed coated with a light plaster. Blackish blubber lips appeared at a hole for the mouth and there were smaller holes for nostrils and eyes. The torso was encased and the forearms, held bent at the elbows, were two thick white sausages with just the fingertips showing.

'Oh Robin, come in, dear boy.' The man walked stiffly, like an automaton. Hood saw he must be showing his horror because Wynyard said, 'Yes, he's one of our bad cases, poor fellow . . . oh, it's all right, he can't hear. He was at Woodham. Shot down four Messerschmitts . . . baled out twice, third time crashed in flames . . . terribly badly burned . . . never been able to get him out of the bandages, poor fellow . . . Still, he manages to do astonishing things . . . Come in, Robin.'

He pointed to Hood and, in dumb show, explained what they wanted. The man seemed to understand, gave a stiff nod. As he turned to go, Hood noticed how tall he was, and broad-shouldered – perhaps it was the effect of the bandages but he seemed to be a very big man. The door thudded to behind him.

'God Almighty,' Hood couldn't help himself.

'Poor fellow. You'll find him very gentle. Another whisky, Mr Hood?'

'Thanks, I don't think I will,' Hood said. 'I'd like to get a car out there. Mine's a write-off. Is there——?'

'I was wondering how you'd got here, to the house.' Wynyard's smile was so mild and kind, his manner so amiable. 'There's only the private road – four kilometres long.'

There was a sudden edge to his voice. The stillness of everything was extraordinary, the stillness of the room, of the whole house, of Mr Wynyard standing there smiling, as if he were listening to one of his spirit voices; and yet, in a strange way, Hood felt that there was something more, just out of his reach . . . that he should perhaps be listening for.

He said, 'I must have got on to the wrong track entirely. I had to come through the fields.'

'Oh, the fields.'

Then the door beyond opened and Sir Harry Belgeorge came in.

For perhaps two seconds, Hood did not recognize him; it wasn't the surprise, the complete overwhelming unexpectedness of the thing – though, of course, there was that – but Belgeorge was dressed entirely in white and Hood had never seen him in anything except the formal black coat, striped trousers, stiff collar and pearl grey tie that seemed to be a sort of uniform with him. Now, with this suit, even his tie and shoes were white. And there was a change in manner.

Belgeorge came forward decidedly, his hair falling romantically on his temples, his face, as handsome as ever, somehow made more genial and sporting by the humour of his smile.

Hood said, 'Good God!'

'My dear Hood, I am delighted to see you. I heard you were here. I see you've met the Air Commodore.'

'Yes.' How had he heard? Hood wondered. And now, of course, his memory jumped the gap – he had seen Air

Commodore Wynyard at Belgeorge's, either a house party or at one of the grave and fashionable affairs to do with The Movement.

'Good lord, are you hurt?'

'It's nothing much,' Hood said. 'Commodore Wynyard's been very kind. I must say I didn't expect to find you here.'

Belgeorge laughed – Hood noticed how perfect his teeth were – 'Nor I you! What've you been up to?'

'A crack-up with my car. Just down the road.'

'Fortunate you were so close.'

'Fortunate I was.' And then the impulse was to tell Belgeorge what had happened, to recruit Belgeorge's powerful help – he or Wynyard would know all the local people and would be able to get him away. The men might still be outside. There was no need to go into the thing deeply – just the mention of shooting would be shock enough for Belgeorge. Belgeorge was standing in front of him, perched forward, smiling, rocking back and forth a little on his heels – the picture of energy.

'Matter of fact,' Hood said, 'it wasn't so much accident as design. Somebody just tried to kill me.'

'What! To kill you?'

'Yes.'

'My dear Hood, you – you shock me beyond words.' It was plainly true – Belgeorge's face had suddenly become ashen, the lines downward, eyes staring. His whole stance had stiffened.

'Oh,' said the Air Commodore.

'Who was it?' Belgeorge said.

'Well, it's a pretty long and circumstantial story which I won't bore you with. I came out from Orly this morning looking for a place called Les Gerfauts.'

There was a brief silence. 'This is Les Gerfauts,' Belgeorge said.

THE MAN ABOVE SUSPICION

T HEY ALL kept very still, as if they were struck by the meaning of that answer. The sun had come out again and the pattern of the windows and the leaves outside was flickering and shimmering on the stone floor. There was a glint from the shield where it had fallen so strangely and the faint smell of Wynyard's pipes in the room. Then Belgeorge said, 'So you have come to your destination, Mr Hood.'

'It seems so.'

'Peter,' Belgeorge turned to Wynyard. 'It will be best if we are left alone. Would you mind?'

'Very well, Harry.' The Air Commodore smiled gently and went out.

'Maybe you can begin by telling me where Miss McCaine is?' Hood said.

'My dear Hood, we must not be sidetracked. Your glass is empty. Can I give you a – whisky, was it? Pray don't move.'

Silently Hood watched him. Belgeorge poured the whisky and added soda, handed Hood his glass, poured sherry for himself and took a swallow. Hood noticed a peculiar brilliancy in his eyes which he hadn't seen before.

'I've always thought of you as a man of culture, my dear Hood – intelligent, sensitive, individual – and so, of course I'm glad we've fallen together as we have. Our aims are the same. We are both travellers along the same highway.

'I don't think anybody with your insight can doubt that we've got to a point where things can't go on as they are any longer.'

'Things?' Hood said.

'Everywhere there's collapse, frustration, bewilderment, despair. In this age, the age of science, we are moving towards a dark tunnel. Don't you agree? The new Dark Ages are coming. Religion, socialism, pioneering, the frontier life, art, democracy – all the things that inspired past generations are dead or dying. Mediocrity sits on the necks of honest men. Responsibility is a whore. The best things in life are easy to get – that's the word. We see the cult of pornography, the mystique of permissiveness. Everywhere morality and the old standards are failing, and the miasma of decay hangs over us. Isn't it true, Mr Hood?'

Hood nodded. It was true enough. He watched Belgeorge's face.

'Public office – you know, it's become a field where fact and truth are minor considerations. The best men are either fighting the system or taking refuge in private worlds. And what do political parties offer? The same calamities. In the countries that had representative government, the basic assumption of political life has been overthrown – that if one side doesn't work, the other will. It isn't so any more. Neither works. And in the others, the political gangster system is falling apart.

'I wouldn't be surprised if we don't soon have the Red Guards of London, the Grey Guards of Paris and Washington, when somebody smart gets holds of these lost young people.

'You remember all those visions of future hells they used to promise us – 1984s, aseptic New Worlds, transcendental cities, double-think and Big Brother? They were all wrong, all wrong. We've got the opposite – rights without duties, without effort, the creeping mania of adolescents, mimicry on an international scale and a life for ordinary people that is terribly trashy and terribly unsatisfying, not only no Big Brother but no brother at all.'

He paused, took a drink. Hood watched him fascinated.

[121

'And the ethos of failure is on the rise again too, you know. Failure's glamorous. If you're a failure, you are somehow great – a success. And people embrace mystic sects, anything to escape; but what about the mass, poor devils, who can't escape and only get the narcotics of the telly? It isn't economic need, people have more material well-being than ever – it's moral despair. They need something in the greyness, if it's only a sense of belonging.

'And men everywhere, you know, Mr Hood, *hate* modern trends. Hate them. Secretly they yearn for the world to turn away from these hideous gods, long for inspiration, a banner to follow. Give us a cause that will exalt us, they shout. Only they don't think they have the power to help bring it about.'

He took another swallow of sherry.

'It's hopeless to think this will change by itself. But the world is ready for our lead and we must not be afraid to assume our responsibilities. The new society, of course, can't be formed by gentle appeals. It has to be fired in a crucible – hardened, tested. A child needs the certainty of discipline, which means punishment, authority, rails to run on, a system it can trust in, rely on, which has its fixed rules for the minor circumstances of life just as it has for the great crises – and so does society.

'Intolerance is the secret of really successful social organization. I trust that doesn't sound cynical to you because of course Christianity itself is founded on intolerance – and I don't mean intolerance of other people but of practices, what you *do* – what the faithful do. Rigour, discipline, enlightened severity, the firm hand, less government not *more* government but of a finer quality – these are what people need. And these are what we shall give them.'

'We?' Hood said.

Belgeorge smiled, ran a hand through his hair. 'You only know The Movement, of course, Mr Hood. That

122]

is the outer envelope, as it were. Within, we have the real instrument – The Brothers.'

His eyes were on Hood's; and Kim McCaine's words on the island came back to Hood. 'They are a group of men . . .' He understood now; they were a secret society.

'All I have been saying to you, Mr Hood, we have proved with The Brothers. Proved it. The Brothers fills the deep needs men have for the things they have lost. We have iron discipline. Every member must protect and shield the others, even to death. No member covets the women of others – and so on. We demand constant sacrifice. And we have found that our austerity in the midst of the general drift and laxity and the vacuum of non-morality is magnetic! Men have flocked to us. Brothers *belong* again, they have purpose, a sense of fulfilment. I have laid it down that, since we should be misunderstood and persecuted – men who make a stand in our day are called fascists (he smiled) – we must temporarily remain secret.

'Above all, we are against violence. We've renounced violence because it breeds violence. That is why, my dear Hood, I was shocked to learn just now that there had been an attempt to kill you. I shall deal with this.'

Hood said, 'You were speaking of solutions. What are your solutions?'

Belgeorge moved across the room, then came back. 'I think we all know the men who must be removed, don't we? It is not so complex, after all, not so difficult in the long run to see the men who are evil. We are agreed, in The Brothers. We have a historical task.

'I'm a believer in the impulse which individuals give to history – that it is individuals, not blind economic or social forces that generate and shape events. Without men like Napoleon, Hitler, Stalin, Mao, the course of the world would have been vastly different.'

The sun came into the room and illuminated Belgeorge's

head – the noble features, the hard intelligence of the eyes, the expression of energy. A man of the highest motives – the most dangerous of any. The one type society still could not cope with was the fanatic – and looking at him, Hood knew that that was what Belgeorge was.

He tried not to show his feelings and lit a cigarette. 'How are you going to remove the people in power if you don't use violence?'

Belgeorge looked at him. 'I cannot, of course, tell you the method. That is secret. As leader of The Brothers, my duty is towards my companions. But we are moving to the phase of action now. Our ideals will remain pure and we shall shun violence because . . . we have a weapon . . . a formidable weapon.'

'But you've just said—'

Belgeorge raised a hand. 'That's all I can tell you.' He went towards the door, turned round. 'And I am glad you are with us, Mr Hood.' He went out.

Hood sat staring in front of him. It was fantastic. A lot of it was true but the answer was mad. Society as a child. Belgeorge saw himself as the saviour, the new messiah. And – Hood gasped as the purity of the white suit struck him – the symbol of Belgeorge's leadership! That was what was terrifying in such men – that what would deter others by its ridicule, its comedy, they took with deadly seriousness – the Hitler moustache, the manic salute and the goose-step and the Nuremberg parades; and not only Germans but manic British generals too, glaring at subordinates 'I'm the Supremo!' And non-violence – the vacuum that always produced violence. He remembered Belgeorge and the Celebes apes at his zoo and their 'natural order' with the dominant males as 'the supreme rank'.

He got to his feet, limped down the room. The door was locked; he crossed to the two others and tried them –

both locked. He examined the window and saw a squaring of fine copper wires set into the glass – an alarm system. His ankle felt worse and he knew he couldn't get far.

As he reached the chair again, the door at the far end of the room opened and a nurse in white uniform came in with a tray of first-aid kit – evidently somebody they kept to attend to the burnt man.

Hood sat down, shaken and preoccupied with Belgeorge's words. He felt exhausted, shut his eyes for a moment, then looked down, feeling a clammy touch on his ankle. The woman was kneeling, bent over his foot and Hood saw she was wearing grey rubber gloves. The tray beside her looked unexpectedly professional – clinical – and on it was a saucer of needles or hypo heads. And suddenly Hood had a feeling of horror and panic. Her fingers in the rubber gloves held a bottle and a pad of cotton wool, a strong smell came from the bottle as she tipped it.

'No! No!' He jerked his foot away from her, pushing back in the high chair and she slowly raised her head and looked up at him. It was the woman toilet attendant from Orly.

Hood shrank back . . . took a grip on himself. He said, 'I'll do it myself . . . just leave me the bandage. Only the bandage.'

Her grey eyes were on him, she said nothing, got to her feet and went out. Hood passed a hand over his face. God Almighty, had he gone mad? How had they brought off the Orly trick? It had been part of the diversion, to keep him away, keep him from going back to that toilet while they were smuggling Kim out.

He limped over to the door by which the woman had left. It was locked. His ankle throbbed heavily. Had she, after all, put something on it? What had Kim said? 'They are going to make something horrible . . .'

He had begun to sweat and he had a slight tremor.

THE BRAIN

14

HOOD LAY tense in bed in the room they had taken him to, listening to the steady rain and trying to distinguish other sounds through it. The rain lasted till dawn when Hood fell asleep. A servant in red striped waistcoat woke him with breakfast and later brought lunch and dinner. When Hood asked for Wynyard or Belgeorge, the man nodded silently but nobody came. The bell-pull produced no response. The door was locked by some electric system because there was no key and it snapped shut immediately the man went out.

It was a big panelled room on the third floor with tapestries, canopied bed and modern bathroom adjoining, and overlooked the garden with its little trimmed French hedges and borders set out in an eighteenth-century pattern. Hood saw nobody down there and the house remained as silent as ever – the whole place might have been deserted except for himself and the servant.

He kept wondering why Belgeorge hadn't spoken of Morell or the island – or tried to find out how much he knew. And how did the death of T. T. Lucas fit in with Belgeorge's profession of non-violence? Was that hypocrisy? Hood didn't believe it. Belgeorge had been in absolute earnest, there had been the brightness of mad faith in his eyes.

On the second morning he heard a heavy truck moving at the back of the house but couldn't see anything; an hour later, there was a faint electric hum . . . a lift working?

The only thing to read was a four-volume work on Hieronymus Bosch and Hood sat with his leg up for hours, looking through the terrible medieval demonology and every now and then renewing the cold-water bandage on his ankle. By the second day the swelling had gone and the ankle was normal, but every time the servant came in Hood made a play of moving awkwardly and painfully. The afternoon dragged by.

Just before eight o'clock he heard the man coming, went quickly to the chair and sat down with his leg on a stool. The man came in, giving him a quick glance. Hood was sitting back exhaustedly. The man put the dinner tray down, turned to take the uncollected lunch tray from the table beyond and Hood snatched up the stool and hit him hard over the head. The man grunted, dropped to his knees, letting the tray go with a crash. Hood hit him again and he fell forward among the plates.

Hood stepped over him and searched him but found nothing. He yanked the bedclothes off the bed, ripped a sheet into strips and tied the man up, pulling a gag tight across his mouth. But fifteen minutes later he was still wrenching at the door, cursing and stripping his broken nails.

How in God did it work? He had watched the man come and go, seen him simply turn the handle and pull or push. The man had come round and was on the floor groaning through the gag. Hood bent over and frisked him again; there were two twenty-centime pieces in his pocket, a handkerchief and not a thing else. He stared down at the man, took the gag off.

'How do you get the door open?'

Weakly the man shook his head. Hood grabbed him by the ears and banged his head on the stone floor. 'How do you open the bloody thing?' The man's jaw sagged but he didn't answer.

Hood got up baffled, gave him an exasperated shove with his foot, rolling him over on his face. Then as he turned away again to the door, Hood did a double-take and swung back.

The man was wearing a big cheap ring of white metal. Hood stood looking at it, then bent down, worked it off and took it over to the door. He touched the doorknob with it. There was the faint metallic sound of electric tumblers tapping up inside and the knob turned. Hood grinned. The ring was a magnet. He slid it on to his right hand, gagged the man again and went out. As he took his hand off the knob, the tumblers fell and the lock clicked shut.

Along the corridor he reached a broad landing and the main stairs down. Cautiously Hood peered over. The hall below, in the failing daylight, was still and silent with the suits of armour making shadows. He went softly down one floor, caught a faint tapping sound like somebody approaching in slippers, cast round and ran along the corridor. An opening showed a narrow stone spiral stair. Quickly he went down and at the bottom stepped out into a bare stone space with pillars and vaulted ceiling that looked like an old cloister, evidently some older part on which the house had been built.

The light came faintly through a grating. On the farther side was a passage and a heavy door. Hood pulled the bolt, eased the door open. Something made a faint skittering sound in the dark and he caught a mingled smell of chemicals and . . . some animal? Water dripped and there was the hum of air conditioning.

Groping, he found the light switch; bright flashes stabbed the dark and he was blinking under fluorescent tubes. He stood staring, slowly walked forward. It was a laboratory. His eyes ranged over deep sinks, tiled slabs and surfaces, gowns hanging on hooks, rubber tubing, bowls and dishes of liquid, nickel boilers, glass cases of instruments. The pulsing body of a small animal, slit open, lay on a slab with tubes from its insides to a machine alongside.

Farther on was a row of wire cages holding rats, mice, guinea pigs, rabbits and two small dogs. Something grabbed his trouser leg and he stepped back looking down at a cageful of rhesus monkeys. A faint gabble was coming from somewhere beyond.

The place was extensive, the whole cloister transformed into this underground lab. It gave him the creeps but he went on. At a recess he checked. There was an oval glass door set in steel, like an oval porthole, with DANGER NO ENTRY painted on it and a steel control box with combination lock fixed to the wall. Inside was a second glass door – it was an airlock door.

He went closer then jolted back. Two gasmasks with protruding snout-like filters swam towards him. Then he saw they were hanging in two plastic bags outside the door with overall rubber suits, boots and gloves. They were sterilized masks and heavy protective clothing for handling toxic substances, hanging there for fresh use–and the airlock door was meant to prevent airborne infection.

By the dim red light through the door he could see it was another lab with substances in shallow trays, massive refrigerators and things that looked like handling tongs.

'We have a weapon . . . a formidable weapon . . .' He remembered Belgeorge's glowing face. This must be the experimental centre where they had produced it – and now they were manufacturing it at the Princess Zherkov plant at Grasse. A laboratory weapon . . . Hood shrank. But their claim of non-violence? It sounded insane.

He turned, looking round the rest of the place. A tap in one of the sinks dripped evenly, the air conditioner hummed, otherwise there was silence. He saw another door in the far corner and went over. As he opened it, the muttering sound he had heard before was louder. A dim red light glowed inside. The muttering died away and he pushed the door wider – another lab. Now he could hear the faint pulsing of a machine and beyond that, hardly audible, the swirl of liquid. He went in.

A terrified scream tore out of the silence. Hood stood against the door, the muttering began again and raced in a gabble of sounds rising to another scream. Hood was stock-still, eyes searching – it was some animal he couldn't see; then his eye caught the grey box of a loud-speaker in an upper corner. A sound relay? He didn't get it.

He stepped forward round a loaded trolley and froze. On the central table was an upright frame of nickel rods supporting two prongs, curved like claws, which between them delicately held a brain. It was a whole brain with fragments of bone left at the temples where the prongs held it. A straggle of rubber tubes, gently pulsing, linked the thing to a tank of blood and a small heart-lung machine alongside. Staring, Hood moved closer. About twenty tiny electric needles stuck in the surface of the brain were connected up to an electro-encephalogram and other instruments.

Hood said 'Christ' aloud – and there was an immediate scream then wild chittering. The brain was alive and the wired-up auditory and speech centres were reacting to him with panic fear. The isolated brain knew he was there; it was screaming with a voice it didn't have, maybe desperately trying to escape with non-existent legs. It was a marvellous piece of advanced neurophysiology – with the touch of Klein, the genius in sound engineering whom Rosario had employed.*

The screaming began to unnerve Hood and in spite of himself he blurted out, 'Shut up! Shut up!' He stood staring at the brain, taken by a mixture of pity and anger he couldn't account for, as if some lost instinct had stirred in him. 'Shut up, will you!'

Momentarily the screams sank to a jabber then rose to panic again. Somebody was going to hear – and then it struck Hood that the speakers could be hitched up elsewhere, relayed to some other part of the building. He turned furiously towards the table, reached for the tangle of tubes to wrench them off, the brain gave a sort of

*See *Shamelady*

130]

barking shout. Something flicked across the light, Hood snapped round, caught the fleeting half-glimpse of a figure behind him and a black bag came over his head and was pulled tight.

He went backwards, struggling and gasping and hitting out until he lost consciousness.

*

He could see nothing. His head throbbed with pain. The pressure on the bones at the temples felt as if his head were held in prongs. He couldn't feel anything else. Sometimes in the dark there were sounds which terrified him, yet he didn't know what the sounds were. Waves of fear swept over him and he screamed. Was he screaming? Who asked the question? Was he a brain screaming?

Electric shocks pricked his head at intervals. He was aware of a rhythmic pulsing but didn't know how he experienced it, just as his experience of the diffuse unreal light was not seeing but vaguely sensing. Sometimes the shocks filled him with wild unknown terrors and he ran . . . ran . . . but couldn't escape. Screams came to him from the void. Were they his own screams?

Then everything was silent, deep spaces of emptiness, with terror poised. The light began to change, there were flashes and he swam up through a fog, intermittently seeing things he felt no relation to – a grey ceiling, dark wallspace, the table he was lying on, rubber tubing which ran from him. Needles were being stuck into his head and his veins.

After another blank period he came up again. This time he saw it was a laboratory; there were voices. Then Belgeorge's face, red with anger, swam into view at the foot of the table and though Hood couldn't hear anything, he could see Belgeorge speaking furiously to someone else, giving orders, pointing at him and obviously telling them to take him away.

Some time after this he felt himself being moved and

next thing he knew was waking up with a morning light coming through the window and Belgeorge standing beside the bed. It was a different room. His head ached but was reasonably clear. Belgeorge, in his usual black coat and striped trousers, was beaming, leaning forward.

'My dear fellow. How are you? Feeling better? How's the head? You kept complaining of your head.'

'Not bad. Damn thirsty.'

Quickly Belgeorge filled a glass of water on the bedside table and handed it to him. 'Ankle fit now too, h'm?'

Hood swallowed the water, nodded. 'How long did your friends keep me under?'

'Oh!' Belgeorge laughed in his attractive, frank way as if he were covering embarrassment – as if they had tacitly agreed to treat an awkward untoward little incident indulgently. 'One of my chaps was interested in – um – your—'

'Brain?'

Belgeorge laughed again, a little more uncomfortably. 'Well, he wanted a tracing, you know, on the electroencephalogram. Collects them. He has his own technique.'

'Collected many?'

Belgeorge chuckled, forcing the bright note. 'He wanted to – um – extend the tests, you know. He's found a new brain wave, he says. Very interesting.'

'I thought at one point I was just an isolated brain on two prongs, like the one he's got downstairs.'

For a flash, Belgeorge's look became icy, then he dragged the smile back again. 'Well, now I'll have them bring you some fruit juice or perhaps some coffee? You'll have time for a short rest but we'll be leaving this afternoon.'

'Yes? Where are you going?'

'Oh, you'll be with us. You'll be with us.' He was looking at Hood with bright intensity. 'I've been speaking to J. D. Morell. He's anxious to see you – my dear – um – my dear Conroy.'

132]

SCHLOSS GRIMMINGSTEIN

15 THERE WERE moments during that bright, late, summer afternoon when Hood thought that they were too powerful, too well organized to contend against with any hope.

The airfield near Tours from which they took off had the look of a military field – there were men in blue uniforms in the distance – and they could obviously not have used it without superior influence. Belgeorge was laughing, confident, good-looking, full of vigour, saluting the deferential group of men there to see them off.

Sitting at the back of the Beechcraft with three guards, Hood struggled against sleep. And when they landed an hour and a half later and stepped out into the cool air with the mountains all round, there was another impressive little scene – men coming forward raising hats and greeting Belgeorge with the respectful formality a big man gets.

Where was it – Germany? Switzerland? Somewhere in the high alps, at all events. Belgeorge was striding ahead with the men, hair blowing in the wind. It was a sports airfield and the sign on the building said Aigen. Austria!

The guards kept close up to Hood as they went through. Cars were waiting outside and took them to a small mountain train and very quickly – again as if everything had been waiting for their arrival – the whistles blew and they were moving, climbing up the valley with the red engine clanking in the cogwheel track and a steward coming in to serve drinks.

Hood took a whisky. He could see Belgeorge in the private car ahead talking with the men who had met them. And again Hood was struck by the emanation of confidence and power – the group of men framed by the glass panel, Belgeorge's profile against the light, his hand poised, turning from one to the other of them as he spoke, and the others, with their eyes on him, listening. He had them spellbound. There was a sort of fervour in the way they listened to him, an expectancy.

The train climbed round sharp curves, in and out of tunnels. In places the rock-face on either side was only inches away. There was no road – evidently the train was the only way of getting up here.

And abruptly the line ended – a simple platform, a line of waiting cars and nothing else. They were high up with the snow peaks everywhere and Hood wondered where they could go from here, then saw the metalled road winding up from the railhead. It must be a private road they had built themselves. An arrowed sign in Gothic lettering said *Grimmingstein*.

The file of cars moved slowly up, they passed a guarded roadblock and then through the pines they were running out across grassy slopes in front of a castle – a mad Styrian king's dream. There were towers, steep slopes of roof, pointed gables. What a setting – worth a finer inspiration than this, Hood thought; and as he looked at it against the void beyond, there was also something primitive and barbaric behind the romanticism.

Groups of men were strolling about. At the head of the file of cars at the entrance, Belgeorge was surrounded, greeting and smiling and shaking hands, then Hood's car peeled off to a side door. The lead escort signalled to him and they marched Hood through to a windowless room and shut the door from outside. Hood could hear their voices.

The room had a table and chairs, a framed outdoor photograph of Belgeorge on the wall with wild prophetic hair. Hood lit a cigarette and sat down. This must be The Brothers' alpine retreat and by the look of things something was in preparation. He felt oppressed and

134]

edgy. As he finished the cigarette and trod on the butt there were steps outside and Morell and Belgeorge came in.

Morell in a blue blazer and cream shirt looked bigger and more athletic than he had on the island. Belgeorge said, 'Is this the man?'

'This is the man. Mr Ed Conroy.'

'Well!' Belgeorge's tone was mild, his look like a man astonished at a friend's lapse. 'What have you got to say?'

'Say?' Hood said. 'What would you expect?'

Morell said, 'You killed three men on St Kilda's and you'll be interested to know that there is a murder charge out against you.'

'I was trying to keep clear of those gun-parties of yours.'

'We also found Novak,' Morell said.

'Self-defence.'

'Who sent you to St Kilda's?'

'You hired me, remember?'

'Who put you on to Conroy?'

'Conroy tipped me off himself, didn't he tell you?'

'Don't give me your bloody lip.'

From the background, Belgeorge put in, 'My dear J. D., is it necessary . . . ?' Morell half turned to flash him a look, turned back to Hood. 'We intend to know.'

'You'd save yourself a lot of trouble, Morell. I wouldn't tell you anything.'

'You think so?' Hood saw the quick little struggle in Morell's face as Morell suppressed his fury, fought himself under control because Belgeorge was there. Morell was standing a pace or two in front, so that Belgeorge couldn't see his expression but Hood's eyes took them both in – Belgeorge, still courteous, distinguished, Morell dark with anger, only checked by expediency.

'I'd advise you to co-operate,' Morell said. 'You were sent in by an oil firm, weren't you?'

Hood slowly took out a cigarette and lit it. He didn't answer.

'You see, we shall have to hand you to the police,' Belgeorge put in.

'The police?' It sounded comic in its incongruity, but Belgeorge nodded.

Morell said, 'The St Kilda's Government is applying for your extradition.'

'You as the St Kilda's Government, of course?'

'We have very close relations with them.'

'Sure,' Hood said. 'And I imagine they've got extradition treaties all over.'

'Sorry to disappoint you,' Morell snapped. 'They renewed the former British ones. It happens to be one of the things they've taken particular care of.'

'But the police here would want a fat report first – on a lot of other things.'

'Such as?'

'Be too easy if I told you, wouldn't it?' Hood said. It was absolute bluff. They looked at him in silence, their eyes searching his face and Hood knew he mustn't by a flicker show how little he in fact knew.

What could he prove against them? Nothing. Long before he could ever tell the police about what they were doing at the Princess Zherkov plant or Les Gerfauts, they would have cleared away all trace. The police at Grasse would find themselves poking about among old-fashioned creams and rice-powder. The accusations against Belgeorge would sound wild – it would be like attacking the integrity of the Lord Chief Justice.

And of course they had all their cover prepared, their influential members on call, the quick withdrawals ready at a moment's danger. His whole experience of them since the island showed their confidence.

There was a buzz at the door and Belgeorge went over and talked in a low tone with somebody outside. He turned back. 'I shall have to leave you. I have people waiting. J. D., will you . . . ?'

'Yes,' Morell said. Then, as an afterthought as Belgeorge went out, Morell stepped quickly to the door and beckoned. Two of the men outside came in. Morell hitched himself on to the edge of the table, looking Hood up and down. His lips were clamped and when he spoke he seemed to prise them open with difficulty.

'Don't worry, we'll make you sing, Mr Hood.'

'Some of those non-violent methods of yours? Like the ones you used on T. T. Lucas, for instance?'

Morell's eyes went blank, then he said, 'We haven't all got Sir Harry's spiritual purity. He sets too high a standard.'

There was just the faintest tinge of sarcasm in the tone and Hood said, 'He wouldn't have to strain much for you.'

'Shut your trap, you bastard.'

Hood cursed himself for having said it. He said, 'Listen, Morell, Miss McCaine had nothing to do with getting away from the island. I forced her to come, took her as hostage. If you've any decency you'll let her go.'

'Don't worry about Miss McCaine. You won't be doing her any good – if you ever could have.'

The temptation was too powerful. Hood jumped in, threw a quick right and connected with the middle of Morell's face. Morell flew backwards, the table went over. The two guards jumped on Hood, one of them smashing with a cosh, the door shot open and more men rushed in. Hood hit out, but between them they overpowered him. Morell got soggily up from the floor, spitting, wiping his bloody nose. He stepped round the table, looked murder at Hood. 'I'll attend to you later. It'll be a special pleasure.' He jerked his head to the men, 'Upstairs!'

They dragged Hood out to a service lift, took him up, kicked him into a room at the back and stood round kicking him for a few minutes before they left. Hood lay

[137

there, then picked himself slowly up, sluiced his head in the washbasin, sat on the bed with a towel to his head, recovering. It was nearly dark.

Presently he got up and looked out of the window. There was a sheer drop down the side of the castle and the rocky pinnacle on which it stood. Not a toehold. He turned to the door; it was about six inches thick with a massive lock.

He sat on the bed, lit a cigarette then stubbed it out, feeling lousy. Morell was obviously going to get him – and quickly. There wasn't going to be any handing over to the police if Morell could help it; the treatment would be much more direct. He thought that slugging Morell hadn't even made any difference to Morell's intentions – and at least he had the satisfaction of not having missed the chance.

Hood nursed his head and his knuckles. Morell would wait until Belgeorge's back was turned, would provide his own explanations for Hood's disappearance. An 'accident' up here, in this isolated place, would be child's play.

Maybe, though, it would be more prolonged and there would be a cardboard box full of fingers to mail to London. It was cool in the room but Hood was sweating. He didn't think he could stand torture and he wondered what he'd do if they asked about Terry Windmiller and Kim. What had they done with Kim?

Belgeorge had suddenly taken on a new aspect, had even become sympathetic – the comparison with Morell, the touch of nobility, made you forget other things. Belgeorge was acting from the highest motives, a pure idealist, above the intrigues of men like Morell —and with his looks, his power with words and this setting, his glamour was undeniable. Of course it was the image they wanted to cultivate – the pure leader. But none of this was going to help him, Hood thought, or Kim.

He felt exhausted and flopped on the bed in his clothes.

*

He woke up cold, blinking in the electric light at three men standing by the bed looking down at him. He recognized one who had brought him up, a big man with an Italian accent.

'On your feet,' the man said.

Hood sat up, his head gonging. 'Where are we going?'

'Mister Morell. You move.' The man coughed.

So this was it. It seemed to be the middle of the night. 'What's the time?'

'We not talk. You move quick.' The man looked nervous. As Hood got off the bed they closed round him and moved to the door. At the end of the corridor they stopped at a lift and the Italian punched the button impatiently several times, checking back over his shoulder and coughing. Finally the doors twitched open, one of them went in first, the other two followed Hood closely. Two floors below they got out, walked down the empty corridor.

Hood's eyes were scouting for a weapon. Ahead of them he saw a console with a heavy lamp on it, tried to ease away a little from the men. Then abruptly the Italian swung round, blocked his path, an open doorway gaped and all together they shouldered Hood into the dark. The door slammed behind him.

Hood got his balance, stood there not breathing, staring into the dark. Not a sound. He extended an arm, groped, touched a marble surface then something small and hard. As he picked it up, a segment of yellow showed beyond as a door opened and the light snapped on. Arm back, Hood saw Terry Windmiller on the other side of the room.

'Christ! Terry——' He tossed the bronze horse he had picked up on to a chair as he went to her.

'Ssh!' She motioned him to silence, pulled him through

[139

into the other room, snapped the key in the lock behind them. It was a bedroom. Hood swung round and looked at her. She was in green silk see-through pyjamas and he pulled her close to him.

'What are you doing here? Are you all right?'

'I'm all right.'

'God, Terry, I thought— You look better than ever.'

'Well . . . so do you.' She looked away but he turned her face towards him again and held her in a long kiss. He felt the warm contours of her back, slid his hand down inside the pyjamas and caressed her hips, the firm round-ness, fingers running into the sweet division behind. Against her he stirred.

She said, 'God, I want you . . .' One of her legs lifted against him, then she disengaged herself.

'You didn't get hurt in that blow-up?'

'Oh, a few bruises. I was lucky.'

'What are you doing here?'

'Don't you remember?' She held out cigarettes, lit them, exhaled a long jet of smoke. 'I'm an old friend of Morell's.'

'Yes, I forgot.'

'Or used to be. I've been crowding my luck lately, though.'

'The three daisies who just brought me down here said they were taking me to Morell. I thought it was going to be curtains.'

'I saw you arrive with Belgeorge this afternoon. I got them to bring you down.'

'That's a hell of a risk to take, kid. If Morell finds out he'll—'

'Oh, it was for me too.' Her eyes held his then looked away. 'Besides, those men do what I tell them . . . sometimes.'

'The big Italian's jumpy.'

'Aldo? He had to say he was taking you to Morell

140]

because of the other two. He's all right.'

Hood looked at her quickly. 'Is he?'

'Yes.' She turned away a little to hide her face. 'He's . . .'

'Do you want a drink?' she said, a shade too quickly — and he pulled her round to him and kissed her fiercely again. Then gently she pushed him away. 'Don't . . . makes it too difficult.'

'I'm sorry — jealous, that's all.'

'Do you want a drink?'

'Please.'

She crossed the room, poured two large whiskies, brought them back. 'We haven't got much time.'

'Do we ever have?'

She sat on the bed. 'If you do what I tell you, you have a chance to make it. It's not a very good chance and you have to leave in twenty minutes.'

'Is this your bargain with the Italian?'

'Not your business!' she snapped.

Hood snatched her wrist — then forced the impulse back. Quietly he said, 'Forgive me . . . it was a lousy thing to say.' He got up restlessly. 'I can't pull out yet.'

'Morell's going to kill you — he missed the chance before and he's not going to wait this time.'

'But I don't *know* enough!'

'If you're trying to find the McCaine girl, I don't think she's here.'

Hood swung round. 'What are these people here for?'

She drew on her cigarette. 'There's going to be a meeting of The Brothers. You know about The Brothers? Well, they're coming in now from all over. Meeting tomorrow.'

'God, I've got to get in, Terry, I've got to hear it.'

'Are you crazy? You're not going to be alive tomorrow unless you go.' She looked at him. 'I knew you weren't Conroy. How did you get into this?'

[141

'I started out . . . I started out trying to find out about a man called T. T. Lucas. There was supposed to be some connection with oil. I didn't know it was this deep.'

She had paled and he said, 'What's the matter?'

'Nothing.'

'Look, Terry – when they picked me up in Touraine, Belgeorge told me a little about The Brothers. I did some scouting on my own and saw the labs there. It's a secret political movement?'

She nodded.

'What are they going to do?'

'Do . . . ?' Her eyes were sombre, she looked away. 'They're going to do a lot of things, if they can.'

'Right now?'

'Right now . . . they're organizing a coup, first in England, then the Middle East . . . maybe Washington . . . if they succeed, in other places.'

'What others?'

'Wherever they can. They're going to take over. They're not so insane. They know the limitations. They've got members all over Europe, in the States. This place, Schloss Grimmingstein, used to be a retreat, they used to come up here for meetings, big men from Europe and the States, talking sociology, politics, philosophy. That's how The Brothers started – how it all started.'

'Belgeorge was head man, the leader?'

'Yes. And they always knew what they were out for – to purge society, get rid of key men whom they thought were evil and replace them. But not with violence – Belgeorge wouldn't have violence. They were rich and they were more and more frustrated, they were getting nowhere – then suddenly things changed overnight. They began to talk about stepping in with "humane weapons " – nerve gas.'

'Nerve gas?' Hood's voice was quiet. 'For the good of society?'

142]

'Chemicals, gases that disable people without killing them. They built labs, started experiments.'

'What – trying to manufacture them?'

'Yes. They had accidents, lost their two best research chemists in a plane crash. You saw that – that man at the château . . . in bandages?'

'The burnt pilot – Wynyard's man? What was he called, Robin?'

'He wasn't burned and he wasn't a pilot. They had an accident in the lab and gave him an incurable skin disease.'

'Christ!'

'They were very well informed. They knew the French had developed a disabling agent called pyrexol which was enormously potent – but they couldn't get their hands on it. They were already watching a British scientist working for the British Government who was crossing to Paris every so often for secret exchanges about pyrexol. He was supposed to be working for the Ministry of Agriculture, that was his cover. His name was Dunlop and they decided to abduct him while he had papers with him.

'They caught him one night in London. For some reason, he didn't leave his papers at Storey's Gate as he usually did and they nearly missed the chance. However, they knew he always went to his club and they had to jump him in the street, intercept him before he got to the door.

'They drove him round in a car and finally made him agree to go back to the hotel for his briefcase. He must have hoped to get away or give the alarm but of course they didn't give him a chance. They went back with him, got his briefcase and took him out the back way through a fire exit.

'Somehow he managed to get a small pocket-size aerosol bomb of a product like pyrexol, which the French had given him, out of the briefcase – either to use on them or to dump. They caught him, there was a struggle and

[143

the bomb spray went off. They were in the car in the Mall. They had to stop, they had one man knocked out, another affected and Dunlop got away in the confusion.

'Luckily they had a second car following and picked up their men. But Dunlop disappeared – he simply hid himself apparently – and when he was found later, about 2 a.m., he was still so frightened he was in a state of collapse.'

Hood said, 'That was the nerve-gas, the effect of the bomb?'

'Yes. They sent a couple back to the hotel for him in case he'd gone back; it was risky but they had his key and they dealt with the daughter when she came back, then pulled out. Everything, except the accident to Dunlop, was very efficiently done.'

Hood racked his brains. 'God, I remember this. The papers said something about a hoax, didn't they?'

'That was the official cover-up. They found the daughter dead in bed next morning and gave it out as heart, though it wasn't.'

'God Almighty.'

'For The Brothers it was complete success. The data in Dunlop's briefcase gave them exactly what they wanted and they've produced a thing called PLS 106.'

'PLS 106?'

'Yes. It's based on something I think they call pyrethric levogine. They knew that when they got what they wanted they would have to have a manufacturing plant, somewhere they could carry on an industrial process without attracting attention.'

'So they bought up the old cosmetics firm, Princess Zherkov?' Hood said.

'You know that?' she said with faint surprise, then went on. 'There were two or three old firms at Grasse going broke, they bought up the oldest. They left everything in place, didn't touch a thing. Everything fitted

144]

beautifully. They needed exactly the same extractors to produce PLS 106 as the old firm had. To make the cover doubly sure, they bought up an insecticide firm which had been using the Princess Zherkov extractors during the off-season.'

'So that's what they're making at Grasse – nerve-gas?'

'Yes.'

'To use in London, Washington, other places?'

'Yes. They are going to remove the key people. The attacks on the various centres, the political centres, army, police, communications and so forth are going to be made with this disabling gas.'

'Good God.' Non-violence. It was mad – even mad enough to succeed.

She said, 'Morell wants to transfer everything to St Kilda's, make it their main base. He says it'll be less vulnerable than Grasse. They've already had a meeting of The Brothers there, at Varuna Reef – what the place was built for.'

'I see . . . They've started to move some of the extractors there. I found them.' Things were falling into place.

'Yes. Morell sent them. I don't think the others know.'

'You mean, Belgeorge doesn't?' He was watching her face. 'How about Belgeorge?'

'Oh . . .' She got up, walked across the room, stubbed the cigarette and took another. 'Do you want to freshen that drink?'

'What? Yes, all right.' It was a curious little break and, holding out his glass, he saw she didn't want to go on. She brought the drink back.

'Belgeorge doesn't like the island idea. He's only gone along with it so far against his will.' She was resisting, as if she had a sort of loyalty to Morell even though she hated him, but Hood pressed.

'How do you reconcile a man like Morell with Belgeorge?'

'Well . . . Morell's simply using Belgeorge. He thinks Belgeorge's political ideas are a joke.'

'Then what's he in this for?'

'Damn it, I don't know!' She flared up, then controlled herself. 'He's got some intrigue of his own, some damned scheme. Belgeorge doesn't see it, *won't* see it. He's above all that. Morell's using him. He's got three men here who are supposed to be from the insecticide firm.' She gave a little shudder but before Hood could pursue it there was a knock on the door and a cough.

Terry stood up. 'That's for you. Please be careful, do what they tell you. And . . . darling, good luck.'

He looked at her. 'Thanks, sweetheart, but I'd rather stay.'

'Charles, *please* go.'

'Can't do it. Besides, what about you?'

'You've got to go – don't worry about me.'

'I never asked you how you got into this.'

Her eyes flicked at him, she turned slowly away, stubbed her cigarette, said with her back half-turned, 'I was going to tell you . . . if I had the nerve. I – I took Tom Lucas to them. They found him making inquiries, getting in too close, put me in his way . . . and he fell for it, poor devil.'

Then abruptly she had swung round and was gripping Hood's arm, pleading and urgent. 'I didn't know they were going to kill him. I swear it. I didn't know they were going to do those terrible things to him – I beg you to believe me, Charles.'

'What did they do?'

'I can't—'

'Yes you can!' He gripped her wrists, staring at her.

'They tortured him . . . then they tied him up alive by a pool in an old zoo on the island. There was a crocodile. It came out of the water and dragged him in

146]

with it. It was terrible.' She covered her face with her hands, racked with sobs.

Hood had a vision of the green-slime-covered pool he had seen in the deserted zoo and a dark snout rising from it and coming towards the bank. He stared at Terry. These things and this lovely girl – how were such connections possible? And she had called Lucas *Tom*, she had . . . Hood struggled with his feelings. Yet, after all, she had not been responsible for what Morell and Co. had done. He took her shoulders. 'It's all right, I believe you, kid. They would have caught him some other way, without you. And you've made up for it since. Look at me – come on, look at me.'

She looked up with eyeblack running. Hood said, 'Don't take it out on yourself. I'm going back upstairs now. Will you find me some way into that meeting?'

'Oh God, Charles . . .' She bit her lip, full of distress. 'They'll find you – they're going to kill you—'

'*Will you?*'

She nodded. 'I'll try.'

The Italian coughed nervously on the other side of the door. Hood stepped over, turned the key and opened it.

AN UNEXPECTED TIGER

16

NOTHING HAPPENED until ten o'clock. The sun was out, the air was crystal and there was a perfect view over the Alps. He felt keyed up and restless, thinking of everything Terry Windmiller had told him last night, these people's mad scheme, the capture of Dunlop, the mystery of Morell's part in it. At ten o'clock the Italian and three other men came in and said Belgeorge wanted him.

Belgeorge was waiting smiling in a little foyer in the basement as Hood and the guards stepped out of the lift. He was in white again and Hood noticed the curious brilliance that his eyes had had at the Château des Gerfauts.

'Good morning, Mr Hood. I'm having to go to a meeting in just a little while but I want to show you something first. I confess I'm – I'm yielding to personal gratification – such is human weakness – but I want you to understand what we're doing. To persuade one's friends is one thing, my dear Hood, to convince one's . . . one's opponents, isn't that much more important, more satisfying?'

'Absolutely.'

They were walking down a passage and at the end went through a door into a big room with a few chairs in front of a glass partition. On the other side of the glass was a big yellowish tiger, a young animal, pacing back and forth. What in God . . . ?

'You see, this is a little demonstration of what we've developed . . . the weapon I was telling you about,' Belgeorge said.

'There's nothing secret about what it's based on. It comes from the pyrethrum flower, Compositae family,

148]

which the Persians were using centuries ago. Darius's soldiers used to grind the flowers to powder, make a paste and smear their bodies with it as an insect repellant – you can look it up in any encyclopaedia.'

Hood remembered the fields of pyrethrum flowers on St Kilda's.

Belgeorge went on, 'The pyrethrum is like a chrysthan-themum, the same genus. It grows in England but has never been of any interest except as a flower. Then a few years ago somebody started growing it in the highlands of Kenya – the altitude is important because it isn't any good lower down – and they found something absolutely startling. They could not only produce four or five crops a year but they got an extract that in a chemical com-pound is enormously potent – far more potent than an in-secticide, something with amazing properties. I'll show you.'

He rapped on the glass, a man came out beyond, nodded, and disappeared again.

Belgeorge said, 'Now I want you to watch the tiger.'

Seconds later they saw a cloud of vapour shoot into the cage. The tiger's ears came round, it stopped pacing, turned its head, sniffing. Then it backed off, lowering its head and brushing a paw over its muzzle. It seemed puzzled, retired to a corner and sat down.

Hood glanced at Belgeorge but Belgeorge was watch-ing the cage, his face intent. There wasn't a sound. Behind them, Hood saw that the Italian and the other guards were at the door. He turned back.

Now the lines of the tiger's body seemed to have changed. The ease and majesty had gone. The animal was no longer resting, but seemed to be cowering, the head and shoulders drawn back, ears flattened, eyes staring.

Then Hood sat sharply forward. A small bald man in brown overalls, the man who had appeared before, was fumbling with the door of the cage. He unbolted it, pushed it open and ducked inside, turning his back while

[149

he bolted the door behind him. Then he pivoted almost comically and faced the tiger.

He looked casual, absolutely unconcerned. The tiger was on his feet, jaws slightly open, staring at him. It let out a rumbling growl and Hood shrank. The man had nothing in his hands, neither a whip nor the usual animal-trainer's chair. He stepped forward and the next minute the tiger was shrinking back, cringing away, terrified and shaking, retreating to the farthest corner of the cage. Its flanks quivered like a whipped dog's.

'Christ!' Hood said – and caught a triumphant chuckle from Belgeorge.

'You see, he isn't hurt. We haven't touched him, he's just frightened and he can't do anything. He's lost the will to fight and he won't even offer defence if the man attacks him. Isn't it amazing, Mr Hood? It alters all our ideas, doesn't it? Now do you see the potential for peaceful change?'

Hood said, 'For God's sake stop it, get that man out of there!'

'I assure you it is perfectly harmless.'

Hood was sweating. Was it possible that Belgeorge had been taken in by the claims about 'war without death'? True enough, the Americans and the French were working on chemical compounds that removed the will to fight. In the early days there had been a N.A.T.O. exercise with troops who had merely been given L.S.D. – they had thrown their rifles away. The French pyrexol was said to have a thousand times the incapacitating power of L.S.D.

But it was unknown territory! The effects were unpredictable. Belgeorge was handling something he couldn't control because nobody knew exactly what the outcome would be with a man – even L.S.D. had unexpected effects and the new substances had never been tried on humans or even other large mammals.

'Get him out!'

'Please, my dear Hood.'

Hood turned aside, he didn't want to see any more. The man was bending close over the tiger. The tiger's head twitched away. The man turned his back on the tiger and came over to the bars facing them, shrugging and grinning, throwing up his hands, making a little act of it. Belgeorge chuckled.

Now the man turned back and walked round the tiger waving his arms. He bent down, picked up the tail and gave it a twitch, then another, then a tug. The tiger tried to slew round, crouching with head down farther into the corner. The man made a comic grimace, crossed the cage, picked up a hunk of gnawed bone and tossed it over scornfully. It landed on the tiger's back and the tiger crawled on its belly to escape.

Belgeorge frowned. 'No, he shouldn't do that. No reason to be cruel to the animal.' He gestured reprovingly to the man but the next moment his face had cleared and he was beaming. 'Well, there, Mr Hood, that's a convincing demonstration, isn't it? You see, the—'

Somebody had come in behind. 'The meeting, Sir Harry. They're just coming in.'

'Oh . . . yes.' Belgeorge turned, hesitated, got to his feet. 'Are we late? You must excuse me, Mr Hood.'

Hood had got up too, Belgeorge began moving towards the door and Hood thought suddenly, why not push through into the meeting with Belgeorge's followers, try to bluff a way in? Through the door he could see more men in the passage.

Suddenly there was a snarl behind them. Everybody swung round. Beyond the glass, in the cage, the man was facing the tiger and as they looked they could see the uncertainty in his face changing to fear. The tiger was on its feet, eyes on him, tail out stiffly behind, its whole body rigid and slightly vibrating.

[151

Very slowly, in slow motion, it began to move towards him, neck out, fixing the man with its yellow stare. It was like a cat stalking a bird.

Slowly the man retreated, touched the bars behind him, began fumblingly and tremblingly to search for the bolt on the door. The fur on the tiger's flanks and spine was bristling. They were all struck motionless, holding their breath as the man got shaking fingers on the bolt, shot it, began to pull the door open.

Then the tiger sprang. The man's eyes bolted, he made a feeble gesture of defence, crashed back against the bars under the weight and the tiger's jaws had his head and it was dragging him back, suddenly flinging him round like a doll, savaging and roaring.

'No! Get him off. Stop – stop it!' Belgeorge's face was quivering, drained of colour.

'Look out, the door's open.'

At that moment, two men ran in beyond, one with a rifle; there was a confused dodging while he took aim, then two reverberating crashes, a third . . . the tiger staggered and rolled over. The man lay motionless, a mangled heap.

Hood's mouth was cindery. Belgeorge was staring, grey and horrified. 'Something was wrong. It was defective . . . It has always worked before. We have done this same thing several times . . . Put out those lights . . . Oh, God . . .' He took out a handkerchief, mopped his face, looked for a moment as if he were going to fall but brushed Hood's hand aside.

'The meeting, Sir Harry.'

'Yes . . . the meeting . . .' He stood dazed for a moment longer then staggered out. Hood stared, too shaken to react, then caught himself and went quickly after Belgeorge, but as he pushed through the door, three of the guards blocked the way. He shouldered forward, they grabbed him, bustled him aside, he could see

Belgeorge disappearing, then as he swung at one of them, somebody hit him hard over the head from behind.

Hood's knees buckled, he felt himself dragged over the stone flags, then they hit him over the head again and kicked him down steps. A door boomed.

He didn't know how long he lay there. Painfully, he got to his feet, catching the amoniac smell of a big animal. There was an iron grille in the far wall with straw underneath it and a dark space beyond. He stood swaying – but couldn't see anything. They had certainly kept an animal here, perhaps the tiger. Maybe there was another behind the grille? He didn't want to look.

Gingerly he felt the back of his head, looked round. The place had a bare stone floor, arching stone walls, two steps up to the door, a single electric light bulb dangling overhead. He couldn't extinguish the image of the man's terrified face, the tiger's jaws crunching on his head. And The Brothers now meeting above . . . God, he had failed after all. Where was Kim? This whole enterprise seemed stamped with disaster.

An hour went by – maybe two, he had no idea. Twice the light bulb flickered and went out for short periods. Gradually he recovered his spirits, threw off the black cloud – nagged to anger by the thought of what was going on above. Maybe they had finished and dispersed? He shouldered the door but hope was vain there.

He paced from wall to wall. The light dimmed with another electric failure and finally went out again. Then as he stood there in the dark, somebody coughed nervously outside the door. Christ! It was the Italian.

A key turned in the lock. In three strides Hood was at the door, eased it open and stepped out. A cigarette glowed away on the right. He turned the other way and ran tiptoe in the dark, one arm outstretched, collided with a door, groped his way through and was going forward blindly touching the wall when the lights came on.

[153

It was the stone foyer by the lift. He sprang up the stairs. At the top was a lobby with a dozen men standing about. Security men looked the same everywhere. Hood walked unhurriedly across to the main staircase and up the first flight to a broad landing dominated by monumental double doors. Arrowed signs said, Executive Committee, Committee A, Drafting . . .

Four more security men were standing to one side and behind the doors he could hear the murmur of numerous voices – the meeting!

As he hesitated, the sound of a commotion came up from the lobby, he glimpsed two of the guards from the basement racing up. He walked to the far side of the landing into a wide arched gallery lined with busts.

Voices came from the landing. He flexed to run, then saw a narrow brown door, half masked by plants, at his elbow. It was ajar, no handle – a service door? He pulled it open, stepped into the dark, pulled the door shut as hurrying feet went by.

Hood couldn't see a thing. Something was humming above his head, his hand brushed a piece of clothing hanging up and next minute he had fished out a torch an was shining it on dthe pair of blue electrician's overalls hanging in front of him.

He looked round – fuse boxes, control panels, switches, dimmers and diagrams of electric circuits. It was the electrical control centre of the building and somebody had evidently just been in dealing with the lighting failure.

He flashed the torch upward. It was a narrow cupboard-like space made of board and plaster, the top invisible somewhere above and had obviously been built into the castle structure fairly recently. He edged along, found an iron ladder fixed to the wall. There was just enough room to climb up.

At the top was an iron catwalk behind a row of spot-

154]

lights with removable panels alongside each spot for servicing. Crescents of light showed round the casing of the spots, he craned peering into the narrow space – and could see the meeting hall below!

Gripped by excitement, he searched for a better place. The windy hum was very loud and now he saw a big ventilating fan working at the end of the catwalk. He cursed – how to stop the thing? – it was deafening. Then he saw a wider gap and looked down.

The austere stone hall, grey with tobacco smoke, was full of men in uneven rows of chairs, turned towards a low platform. Six bronze chandeliers all blazing hung overhead and round the walls were antlers, tapestries of mythological gods, heavy drapes, statues of horn-helmeted Germanic heroes which the spots were intended to illuminate. The white-clad figure of Belgeorge stood out startlingly on the platform.

There was something barbaric in the scene, Hood thought. The frustrated poor had been the world's extremists not so long ago. Now the extremists were the frustrated rich – and their spirit had found its perfect setting here among the legends, the blood-bonds and the stone severity of Schloss Grimmingstein.

He gazed down. Belgeorge was on his feet speaking but something had happened to him. The old easy manner had gone, he looked strained and flushed. Somebody interrupted, Hood saw Belgeorge falter and stop, then several men were on their feet at once arguing. What was happening? Hood strained to hear over the noise of the fan but couldn't catch anything. He watched.

Now Morell was up, the other men gave way and Morell turned, addressing the gathering, emphasizing what he was saying with punches of his right hand. When he sat down, a section of the audience applauded strongly. On the platform, Belgeorge half rose, sat down again, poured water into a glass and drank. He was obviously

[155

distressed and it was something other than the accident with the tiger.

What was going on? Belgeorge wasn't holding them . . . he had lost his grip. Two men made their way over to Morell and leant over his chair talking in his ear. Morell nodded, there was a little group round him. Morell seemed to be leading some outflanking move.

A man at the back was on his feet. Hood saw Belgeorge shake his head several times while the man was speaking. When the man sat down, Morell and his section clapped vigorously. Movements of indignation rippled the ranks near the platform. It looked like a split. Hood groaned that he couldn't hear. All at once, Belgeorge was up again and speaking, demanding quiet.

They let him have his way, Hood clenched his fist with frustration, straining to hear – and then abruptly Belgeorge finished. The clatter and scrape of chairs came up as everybody got to their feet, attendants came in, the doors were thrown open and the whole gathering began to mill around and intermingle, some filing slowly out. An attendant carried a white notice to the platform and propped it up. RECESS 30 minutes.

Hood turned away with a curse and swung the torch beam, searching for a possible way out up here; but the space was only meant for serving the spots and he had to go down again. A hubbub of voices and the occasional clink of glasses came through from the gallery outside where a crowd of them were obviously standing about. Somebody had only to come in to check the fuses again and he was caught.

He went through past the ladder to the far side of the space and found an electrical store with pigeonholes and another door, locked. This side was quiet and the keyhole showed another passage outside. In one of the pigeonholes he found a heavy screwdriver, turned to the lock, then paused.

Somebody was speaking close to where he was, the muffled voice came through. He listened at the door; silence, he lifted his head looking round for the source of the voices, then put his ear to a blank space on the store wall. Two or three men were speaking on the other side, then he heard Morell. '. . . all that's taken care of . . . our operating schedule . . .' The voice faded as Morell moved away from the partition. They were next door.

Hood turned to the door, jammed the screwdriver in and forced the lock. The passage outside was empty. Quietly he ran past the next room to the door beyond, put his ear to it, tried the handle – it was locked. He worked the screwdriver against the lock, gave a shove – and jumped urgently forward to catch the door as it shivered open.

It was a room with polished table and chairs and a door to the next room. Hood tiptoed over.

17

MORELL WAS speaking. 'He's got to give way now – Wiltshur and Meissner and their friends are for it and that settles it. All that's holding us up now is the St Kilda's end, they're not ready yet. We're going to press forward there now and not stop till the transfer's complete.'

This was evidently about the transfer of The Brothers' operating headquarters to the island – what the split at the meeting had been about. Gently, Hood turned the doorknob, opened the door an inch. Morell, wearing a dark blue suit, was hitched up on the table edge, one foot swinging, hand in trousers pocket, cigarette in his mouth – an attitude of relaxed confidence – and standing facing him were a big florid man about fifty with thick yellow hair and a cigar, and a slim younger man with a blue chin, looking quiet and dapper.

The big man's belly shook with a bout of coughing which muffled the words he spoke and Hood didn't get it. Quietly Morell said, 'Look, it's simple. Take New York. We advise the Mayor and the State Governor that there is going to be an outbreak of anthrax in, say, Queens next week unless they pay a hundred million dollars in gold to a Swiss bank to be named by us. The transfer will be a bank transaction – maybe a central bank – so we shan't be hauling any ingots around or any of that. Maybe they'll want to put it through a bullion dealer – comes to the same thing. It'll be transferred to a numbered account, no names, and we have a thick screen of nominees behind that.'

His voice was soft and Hood had to strain to catch the words.

'We don't think they'll do anything when they get the

first warning. So we start a small outbreak as promised. The epidemicity of anthrax isn't very high but it'll scare them. Then we tell them we're giving them an outbreak of, say, psittacosis in some other area, say Brooklyn or on the New Jersey side, just to show we mean business.'

'Psittacosis, that's the bird disease?'

'You can call it that. Birds harbour it. Gives you fever. We have a virulent, quick-acting strain. If they delay payment, we tell them they're going to get another outbreak elsewhere of something worse – glanders or smallpox. Glanders'll kill off the domestic animals, so it will affect the food supplies.

'We communicate strictly with the authorities and nobody else – that'll increase the fear element among the people and give the officials an easy way out because nobody else will know we are on the end of it. At the worst, it will look to the man in the street like a set of natural calamities, the authorities will be able to keep mum and even come out of it with chins up and public pats on the back all round.

'We tell them that they'll go on getting these limited outbreaks until the deal is cleared and we have disposed of the gold. If they try anything funny, we make a more serious attack.'

'What's your delivery system?' the big man said.

'Air, road, agents on foot, it'll vary. You get a Cessna with a bathtub of anthrax spore over Manhattan or cultures of melioidosis dropped in a few cinemas – and they'll talk business.'

The big man said, 'Using the air's vulnerable. They could trace it, block us.'

'Look, Willis,' Morell sounded as if he had already gone over all the objections. 'To deal with this thing, to block an attack for sure, they'd have to close down the entire air system over New York – indefinitely. At the very best, taking a risk, it'd disrupt air traffic all through the New York, Washington, Pittsburgh triangle. It'd mean business chaos. The airlines just won't understand what's happening unless the authorities want to talk – and I'm pretty damn sure they won't, if it's only to avoid public panic. So there's going to be tremendous pressure on them to pay. When they've had one or two outbreaks, nasty killing outbreaks, do you think they'll be able to hold out – to keep a city like New York living on its nerves, waiting for another? They're going to pay. A hundred million will be nothing. Especially as they're not going to lose face. No heads are going to roll. It'll be cheap at the price!'

The big man said, 'You could wipe out that goddam place and the goddam intellectuals ten times and I'd applaud.'

The other one said, 'London after New York?'

'Yes,' Morell said. 'New York first, London next. We use the same technique for London. I want to run a small operation over Nassau, Bahamas after that – then we take it from there. Maybe Latin America?'

'How much of this – this material have you got?'

'We have enough stockpiled and we'll have more at St Kilda's as soon as the transfer is complete.' Morell drew on his cigarette, his leg swung. 'If they're recalcitrant we have some very powerful persuaders. Maybe even a little too powerful.' His voice had dropped to a whisper and Hood could barely hear.

'Yeah?' the big man said.

'*Clostridium botulinum*, the organism for botulism. Kills seven out of ten infected. No immunity, therapy's very difficult and it vanishes without trace in the open air in twelve hours.'

Hood heard somebody in the passage behind but he didn't move from the door. Morell was saying, 'We have a little stock of pneumonic plague which we shall increase when we transfer to St Kilda's.'

'You have it now?' the big man said. His voice was low too.

Morell nodded. 'And something . . . better than anything . . . or should I say worse – vervet monkey disease. Fatal, no cure known.' He paused, looking from one to the other of the men. It was absolutely quiet in the room. 'We don't *have* to use it. We can leave a sample, say, in Hyde Park and tell Scotland Yard to pick it up as proof we've got what we say. What government would take a chance with that for a hundred million pounds? Especially if there were no public disgrace, secrecy guaranteed? That's the beauty of it. We guarantee nobody will know, the government just puts the money down in the secret service credits or some other account that's never probed and nobody's the wiser!'

Hood said, 'Christ!' under his breath. Now at last he understood. It had been Morell who had deluded Belgeorge about 'war without death', sold him on the PLS 106 and the acquisition of the cosmetics firm. Anybody with the capacity for producing an efficient insecticide could produce deadly chemical substances – this must have been Morell's original idea and somewhere along the road he had left it and turned to bacteria.

The animals Hood had flown to the island, the few pens at the old zoo, had been for experiments . . . or for breeding diseases. Now at the meeting Morell had engineered the split to get the transfer to St Kilda's approved – obviously most of his supporters didn't know what his real purpose was. The two men in the room with him now had evidently already been recruited.

Morell was saying, 'We're keeping them sweet in Beirut and Algiers and a couple of other places where the money market doesn't ask questions. Maybe we'll use Cairo for the gold too – all that side is wrapped up. Trace-proof.'

A phone on the table behind Hood buzzed startlingly.

Hood saw the three men's heads turn as he shut the door but he dared not let go of the knob in case they noticed it and he hung there holding his breath. Then he gingerly released it, flattened against the wall – if they came out he would have to break for it. The buzzing persisted. One of them pulled the door open – and the phone stopped.

'Let it go, Osman,' the big man's voice said inside. 'This is important. Go on, J. D.' The door shut again.

Quickly, Hood put his ear to the crack again. Morell was speaking very softly and Hood only got the end of the phrase. '. . . I'm meeting them in London tomorrow and we're setting up the London operation, get preparations. . . . Covent Garden . . .'

Then a voice behind Hood said, 'I thought it was in here,' and he whipped round. Two men were just pushing the door from the passage, they stopped, seeing Hood, and stared uncertainly.

Hood moved forward, holding up the screwdriver. 'Another damn short. If they don't get this wiring renewed pretty soon, I'm not going to be responsible. Excuse me' – he pushed past.

They looked at him in silence and he strode down the corridor hearing them mutter something and enter the room. At the end, he turned the corner, broke into a run and reached a lobby with stairs up and down.

Oh God, if he could find Terry's room . . . The murmur of voices came from the gallery which communicated somewhere on his right. He went fast up the stairs, checked abruptly – there were more groups above, he could see legs and backs. He retreated to the lobby, cast round, pushed open the door ahead – a big panelled library, empty after repainting, with only carpet, curtains and bookshelves. As he swung out again, he tripped on a corner of sheeting spread on the floor outside over a dump of painters' gear left there.

He pulled up. Then he was staring down at the white

strip of calico, obviously laid by the painters, running down to a door in the vestibule below. Wait a minute . . .

He jumped down the stairs three at a time, yanked open the door – an improvised paint store. He stood staring in at the paint, petrol, spirit, varnish – enough material for a dozen petrol bombs or a good fat fire. Christ, though, it was a risk if they had Kim McCaine in the building . . . yet it might also give her a chance to get away.

He grabbed a wad of newspapers and two big cans of petrol and ran upstairs. Standing back close to the wall, he checked round. Nobody. He slopped the petrol round the library, doused the curtains, went down again. Quickly he uncapped half a dozen cans and bottles in the store, kicked them over, then he stepped outside, lit a ball of paper and threw it in.

There was a woof and flames billowed out. Hood raced for the stairs. At the library door he lit another torch and threw it in, pulled the door to. From under the sheet, he snatched a bottle of spirit and a can of varnish and ran under the arched opening to the left. A passage led to a vestibule with antlers, heavy drapes and a carved wooden staircase up. He sloshed the spirit and varnish around, lit a fireball and the drapes ignited.

Had the meeting resumed? He ran down the broad corridor ahead of him, past another opening and at the end reached a carpeted reception room. There was an unattended desk at one side. Hood went cautiously across, opened the big door on the right. It was a handsome office with tall, arched, chapel-like windows looking out on an interior courtyard, deep chairs and a desk. Hood's eyes took in the drinks tray, the portrait of Gobineau on the wall, the door on the far side. There wasn't a sound.

He stepped in – there must be a way through the suite – and was halfway across when Belgeorge came silently through the door and stopped, facing him. His chin was high, his hair was a little disordered and there were shadows under his eyes but he had obviously recovered himself. He was quiet and tense, watching Hood.

'What do you want here?'

'I was just passing through.'

Belgeorge made a sudden movement for the desk, Hood jumped forward and reached it before Belgeorge could touch the bell-push. 'Don't do that,' Hood said. He yanked the big screwdriver out of his pocket, nodded to the door through which Belgeorge had just come.

'Who's in there?'

'Nobody.'

'Be a mistake to lie.'

'I do not lie!'

Hood signalled with his head. 'Lock this other door.'

Belgeorge hesitated then came round the desk and Hood walked with him to the door from the reception room, watched him lock it. Belgeorge turned. 'This is my office. I dislike intruders. What do you want?'

His manner had changed; the fight at the meeting had made him drier, more incisive.

Hood relaxed. 'Sit down. Have a drink.'

'Thank you, no.'

'Mind if I do?'

'Help yourself. I hope this will not be long. I have to resume an important meeting.'

'The quicker the better for me,' Hood said. He poured a slug of brandy from the bottle on the tray and took a swallow. 'You don't like violence, Belgeorge, nor do I. But I promise you'll get it unless you tell me where Miss McCaine is.'

'Miss McCaine?'

Hood looked back at him. If it was acting it was masterly. 'Miss McCaine's a friend of mine . . . and acquainted with Mr J. D. Morell. She was abducted at Orly airport and she's probably a prisoner here.'

Sitting at the desk, Belgeorge looked at him expressionlessly and Hood thought: By God, he's a fraud or he's controlling himself marvellously. He saw Belgeorge's hand go into the open top right-hand drawer of the desk and said, 'Don't do anything rash.'

Belgeorge's hand came out holding a box of cigarettes, he flipped it open, pushed it across the desk. Hood said, 'No thanks.' Belgeorge took one, lit it – Hood had never seen him smoke before and he thought Belgeorge was giving himself time to think. Still watching Hood, Belgeorge reached for the phone, lifted the receiver. When the operator answered, he said, 'Give me Miss Schneppenhorst.'

A voice crackled in the receiver and Belgeorge said, 'Where is Miss McCaine?' There was silence at the other end then the voice spoke a few words. Belgeorge said, 'Have her brought here to me . . . Yes.' He hung up.

Hood said, 'If you're pulling something I can promise it'll be the last time.'

Belgeorge's face had gone death-white.

18

BELGEORGE SAT upright in the chair, his mouth tense, the terrible pallor on his face. Hood swallowed the rest of the brandy in his glass, poured another – and even then, some perverse liking for Belgeorge made him itch to tell him about Morell. But of course he couldn't – a hint that it was out and Morell would cover up like lightning.

They waited in silence. Then somebody knocked at the door. Hood jerked his head and Belgeorge got up and went across. As they reached the door, Hood said, 'Hold it. Stand there.' Hood stood close up to him with the screwdriver over Belgeorge's kidneys. 'Don't make any mistakes. O.K. – open up.'

Belgeorge turned the key and opened the door – and Kim was there outside between a tall masculine-looking woman with a heavy face and a younger man in a blue suit. Kim gave a little gasp at seeing Hood and Hood caught her arm, drew her into the room. 'It's O.K.'

The woman was looking Hood over as if she were confirming a suspicion. The man said to Belgeorge, 'This is correct, sir, you wanted this——?'

'Quite correct,' Belgeorge said. 'That is all.'

The woman's eyes went rapidly from Belgeorge to Hood, then under Hood's prods Belgeorge was shutting the door in her face. *They were obviously going to warn Morell at once.* Hood thrust a hand out, locked the door and snapped round, pulling Kim in front of him so that he could see Belgeorge over her shoulder.

'Kim, are you all right?'

'Yes, I didn't know you were here.'

'Where'd they keep you?'

'Somewhere down below, in a half-basement. Something's burning outside, we could smell it as we came up. You can smell it here now.'

He could feel her trembling slightly against him. He gave her a rapid glance; she was wearing a brown skirt and jumper, the light from the window touched her face and she looked scared but very pretty. Softly Hood said, 'Go over to the desk and get yourself a drink, we're going to have to get out of this place quick.'

She turned, went hesitantly past Belgeorge, poured herself a brandy and drank it with a little shudder. Belgeorge was standing motionless and pale – then abruptly an alarm bell began to ring outside. God Almighty, Hood thought, about time!

'What's that?' Kim said.

Hood stepped up to Belgeorge. 'Lead the way out.'

'Of course not.'

'I've got nothing to lose. Do you want this in the liver?' He dug Belgeorge with the screwdriver. Hood's eyes were cold. Belgeorge's face tightened, he stood there an instant longer, then turned stiffly to the door behind. As they went through, steps drummed across the reception room on the other side, somebody tried the door then rattled the handle. 'Sir Harry, are you there? Fire . . . Sir Harry . . .'

'Move!' Hood jabbed the screwdriver in his back, keeping a grip on Kim with his free hand.

The room beyond was a smaller office with two desks and typewriters, they went through a door on the farther side and came out into an open waiting area for visitors. Now the smell of burning was strong and they could hear many voices. The gallery beyond, grey with smoke, was full of men pressing forward to the main entrance.

A man at the rear of the crowd was attracting attention, gesturing back towards a recess. The crush of men ahead began turning back towards them, some sighted Belgeorge. Running steps were coming from behind.

Hood grabbed Kim tighter and ran past Belgeorge for the recess. Belgeorge called out, 'Stop him!' One man lunged forward, Hood tripped him then they were at the recess, pushing through the glass-topped door to the park outside and running like mad across the gravel. A group of four big black Mercedes was standing parked a hundred yards beyond, Hood sprinted for them, dragging Kim with him and they threw themselves into the nearest car.

As the engine roared they saw three men belting across from the building with Belgeorge among a crowd of others at the door, pointing. Then the car jumped forward, they zoomed across the gravel down the drive, swerving past other groups, suddenly seeing the mass of men milling around at the main entrance in front of them.

Hood swung the car on to the grass verge and slalomed among them, swung away to avoid the line of parked cars beyond and they were on the drive again, curving through the trees with the castle behind them and the road ahead.

Hood stared through the windscreen, lips tight, concentrating everything on the road ahead. Kim was silent beside him. Once she reached out and touched his arm but he didn't look round. There was the roadblock ahead and they would have phoned down from the castle.

The descent was steeper than he had thought, he threw a rapid glance back at a bend but couldn't see anything behind. As he said, 'Duck down,' the roadblock came in sight ahead, a pattern of concrete blocks set in the roadway at a curve with the guardhouse built alongside under an overhanging rock.

Hood grit his teeth, slowed to walking pace. A man in uniform came out of the guardhouse, watching them. As Hood swung the car among the first blocks, he heard a phone ringing in the guardhouse. He twisted the wheel to negotiate the next set of blocks; the man was twelve feet in front of him and the phone had stopped ringing – somebody had answered.

Out of the corner of his eye, Hood saw a second man appear in the guardhouse doorway and call over to the first. Hood wrenched the nose of the car round into the gap, trod down, the man leapt aside, there was a clanging grind as the rear of the car hit the concrete post, slewed round and was held fast.

He accelerated brutally, nothing happened, he turned the wheel, something gave and they were free, swinging madly round the curve beyond.

Hood said, 'Christ!' A minute sooner! The fire must have stopped them getting to a phone. 'Watch out behind, sweetheart.' Kim got up, knelt on the seat looking through the back window.

Something astern was clanging on the road. The rough stony ground at the side of the road was cleared for about a hundred yards on either side to the edge of the forest. They ran down for ten minutes and Hood thought grimly that there was still the train in front of them. There were bound to be people serving The Brothers at the railhead. Kim had turned back and he could feel her look on him.

'What's the matter?' Kim said.

Hood forced a grin. 'Everything's fine. See if there's a cigarette in that glove pocket.'

While she rummaged, he saw two cars on the loops below. They were still a good way down, but coming up fast. Hood cast desperately round, said, 'Hold on!' and swung the car off the road. The wheel spun out of his hands as they hit the stones and bounced, he grabbed it and wrestled the car between tree roots and rocks as they went bouncing and lurching over the hillside. At the edge of the trees there was a faint track. Now he could hear the other cars somewhere beyond. He forced the car into the track with the undergrowth pressing against the sides and slashing the windscreen. They crunched into a hollow, a wheel span, Hood revved the engine and they

crawled up the other side. All at once the path widened
and he accelerated.

They crossed another track, kept going and after ten
minutes pulled up. Hood switched off and they sat listening. There was the hum of insects, an occasional bird,
apart from that the silence of the forest all round.

'Where are we?' Kim said.

'Well, if it's any consolation, this is some of the finest
hunting country in Europe.'

'It's at least appropriate,' she said and Hood grinned.
He lifted her chin and kissed her.

She said, 'The thing is to find the inhabitants.'

'If we find a hunting castle it'll be shut at this time of
year and there's nobody else except the game wardens
and a few hard-up peasants.'

She had found cigarettes, they hungrily lit one each
and he drove on. There were clearings with stacked
wood, an occasional hut, all shut. Whenever they hit one
of the regular forest routes, Hood crossed it quickly,
keeping to the secondary tracks. Twice they saw deer disappearing ahead. The tracks climbed and dipped, faded
until he had lost them, then grew again. They drove for
nearly an hour, Hood saw a place they had passed before
and realized they had circled. How far were they from
Schloss Grimmingstein?

He sat forward, concentrating on the track ahead and
presently they were among outcrops of rock that they
hadn't seen before. Then as they ran steeply downhill,
Hood felt the nearside back tyre grinding on the stones
and at the same moment Kim called out, 'Puncture!' He
let out a curse. They ran to a halt and got out.

'Hey, look,' Kim said. Just ahead, the trees stopped
abruptly, there was a large clearing and a crossing of two
forest routes. They could see the buildings and patches
of cultivated ground of a small farm. Closer in was a
substantial wooden house with decorative carving and a

pair of elk's antlers and several smaller pairs nailed up outside.

'That's the game warden's,' Hood said.

'Oh, thank the lord,' Kim said.

Then as they went forward, they saw the big black Mercedes a little way from the house and five men standing, speaking to the game warden.

19

Hood grabbed Kim's arm. 'Move back. Slowly.' Without turning they retreated. In the cover of the trees, she clung to his arm. 'Oh God . . . it's them.'

Hood threw a glance behind at their immobilized car, it was only just out of sight and somebody entering the track would see it at once. Too bad. They stood watching the group. The game warden, a tall, chesty man with a hat, turned gesturing, evidently explaining the forest routes.

'We have to keep clear of him,' Hood said.

The group stood there talking, one of the men looked as if he were giving the warden orders then they trooped back to the Mercedes and drove off. The warden watched a moment, turned back to the hut and disappeared.

'Darling, what are we going to do?' Kim's voice was scared.

'We have to try to find the farmer. That warden bird's no good. Come on, stick close to me.'

A dog began barking somewhere. Keeping to the trees they skirted the clearing and stopped, looking out at the two-storey wooden farmhouse with the balcony round the first floor. There was a risk the farmer would turn them over but the likelihood was he was under the warden's thumb, depended on him for favours, even for the plot he cultivated, and hated his guts. Anyway, it was a chance they had to take. Hood lined up the house with the warden's, said, 'Ready? Now – run!'

They ran across the small vegetable garden, now seeing the dog pulling frantically on its chain ahead of them and as they came up to the house, a plump, red-faced girl in a black apron came out and stood staring at them. Hood and Kim ran up. The girl turned on the dog, it subsided to growls and turned back, facing them.

They took in the snub nose, thick lips and mongoloid eyes – a defective, yet there was something sharp and almost furtive in her look. She stood gazing back at them, taking in everything, then suddenly jerked back with a gap-toothed grin.

Hood said in German, 'Is the farmer here?'

She stared, mouth open, beamed again, her eyes shining with malice.

'Who's the man here?'

She made an incomprehensible sound, suddenly tilting her head over on one shoulder.

'Can't be anybody else at home,' Hood said to Kim. He gestured to the girl, 'Can we come in? In house – us?' She stepped back, gesturing delightedly and Hood muttered, 'Thank God for that.'

It was a kitchen with an open hearth, pots hanging over the fire, table and wooden bench. When they sat down, the girl clapped her hands with joy and Hood made another attempt at communication. All at once her manner changed, and she ran outside. Kim said, 'Let's go, Charles. I don't trust her. She'll go and tell somebody and those men are coming back.'

A shadow flicked across the window, they were both on their feet and a man came in. It was obviously the farmer, a thickset man in his fifties with a brown, weathered face and pale blue eyes. A *gamsbart* – a little plume of chamois fur in a silver holder – curled forward over his hat, his jacket had green epaulettes and there were green stripes down the seams of his trousers. He glanced at Kim, back at Hood. Hood said, 'We got lost in the forest and we want to get down to the railway. Can you help us?'

'How did you get here?' Hood barely understood his accent.

'Car. We broke down.'

'I will tell the warden. He can help you.'

'We don't want to trouble the warden.'

'He is in charge, he will help you.'

Hood said, 'We've come from Schloss Grimmingstein.'

Pause. The man looked at them. 'Some men have been here inquiring.'

Hood nodded. 'We just saw them go. We want to get down to Aigen or Schladming.'

'There is only the train.'

'Can you take us to it? I'll see you are well repaid for your trouble.'

The man looked at him, weighing it up. Finally he said, 'You will have to wait until dark, otherwise the warden will know I am gone.'

'Thank you.'

'What is he saying?' Kim said.

'It's O.K., he'll take us to the train.'

The man led them to the next room. There was a big tile oven, a table with benches, a faded photograph or two in heavy frames on the walls, a holy picture, a loud-ticking clock. The wooden floor creaked at every movement they made. The man said, 'Wait here. Do not go outside.'

So they waited through that long afternoon with the loud spondee of the clock making everything else quieter and sharpening the sense of some old tragedy, the emptiness of the house, the absence of a woman. It made them more aware of the forest all round and the men searching for them, the warnings that would have been sent to the railhead and beyond to Aigen. Once they caught the sound of car doors slamming and Kim put her hand on his but nobody appeared.

'Do you think this man's all right?' Kim said.

'Yes, I wish I knew where the girl was though.'

Occasionally they heard the rattle of the dog's chain outside and Hood got up and looked. The dog, of course, would know the warden too well to bark, so they would get no warning – and, thinking of this, he suddenly

174]

clapped hands to his pockets; he had left the screwdriver on the seat of the car.

They sat talking softly. The light changed, shading into the greyish-blue of forest light and Hood got the sense of foreboding that dusk always brought. The whole conspiracy of The Brothers seemed less fantastic, became threatening and urgent – who knew how deeply they had penetrated with their influential men everywhere in Europe and America? And Morell's scheme seemed terrifyingly easy to accomplish.

At last the dog's chain rattled again and the farmer came in. 'My daughter is not here?'

'No. She hasn't been back.'

The man looked uneasy. Hood said, 'Has she gone to the warden's?'

'It is possible. The warden has been away, some more men came. He has just returned.'

Kim's look showed she had caught the uncertainty and Hood said, 'It's all right, sweetheart. We're going to get moving.' To the man he said, 'Can't we start?'

The man considered. 'Please wait here. I will go and see.' Outside they heard him call, 'Crescentia! 'Crescentia! . . .' but there was no answer. Ten minutes later he came back. 'The warden has gone again. It is best we go now.' He crossed the room, lit the lamp on the table with care, then outside he took a stick and unchained the dog.

'Don't we need a light–a lamp or something?' Hood said.

'There will be a moon soon. I will take you a short way, a little more than three kilometres.'

Hood said, 'Can we by-pass the terminal and go to the second station down the line?'

'That will be five kilometres.'

'We can make that.'

'Very well, but we must hurry, there are only two trains after dark.'

[175

Hood gripped Kim's hand and they followed the farmer round the house and adjoining stable. They stood for a moment in the shelter of the building scanning the surroundings, then the farmer beckoned them on and they hurried across to the trees.

It was nearly dark in the forest but the farmer struck a path at once and they went forward, Hood and Kim two paces behind. Presently they got used to it and when it was absolutely dark they could sense the man's back just ahead and hear the dog sniffing and rustling faintly through the leaves, and since they didn't fall behind, the farmer increased the pace.

They crossed several forest routes, once they saw headlights in the distance, swinging searchingly through the trees and farther on they checked under cover at a crossing while a car went quietly by. The car moved slowly, they could see the men inside and heard the faint crackle of short-wave radio. The farmer made a small sound and the dog stood rigid. When the car had gone they ran across the route, seeing the moon beginning to rise.

'How are you doing?' Hood said to Kim.

'I'm all right,' she said, in a small voice.

Once the moon was up the going was easier. The man kept away from clearings, then away to the right they could see electric lights sparkling through the trees.

'What's that?'

'The station, terminal.'

'Good.'

They were already a little beyond it, about a hundred yards on, when the man halted abruptly and signalled to the dog to be quiet. Kim moved close to Hood's side and peering ahead they could see the silhouette of a blacked-out car on the track a little way ahead and Hood caught the glint of a rifle-barrel.

'A little night shooting,' Hood whispered. 'Permission of the game warden.'

The farmer turned back and they made a detour round the place. Hood felt Kim beginning to slow up and once or twice the farmer had to stop and let them catch up. 'Please hurry.'

Then abruptly the down gradient became steeper and they saw more lights below them. Fifteen minutes later they were at the edge of the trees, looking across at the small deserted platform in the moonlight, the balconied wooden building with the sign *Wirtshaus zum Bahnhof* and the lights of a few houses beyond.

Hood said to the farmer, 'What's your name and the locality where your farm is?'

'Johannes Walter. Am Hiaslbauer auf der Huben.'

'Thank you, Herr Walter. You are a good man and we're very grateful to you. My name is Charles Hood from London and you will be hearing from me.' He held out his hand and the man took it with a dry nod.

'Thank you,' Kim said, then she leaned forward and kissed him on the cheek. The man looked at her and gave the ghost of a smile. 'Do not go on to the platform now. Wait until the train comes then run to it.'

'Yes.'

'Goodnight.'

'Goodnight and thank you.'

Walter whistled his dog, turned away and disappeared in the dark. The moon shone on the rails and the station and the forest-covered slopes beyond. They moved in closer and stood waiting in the shadow of a hut. Hood put his arm round Kim's shoulder. Then they saw a man in a uniform and a red cap come out of cabin on the platform and the next instant they could hear the train coming.

Hood grabbed her hand. 'Come on!' They ran across the intervening space, seeing the lighted carriages appearing and pulling up. They went through a gate in the low fence, found the way up and ran on to the empty platform as the station-master turned to lift his flag. He shouted something, Hood yanked a door open, pushed Kim in and jumped in slamming the door as the train began to move.

There was a squeak of brakes and the train jolted to a halt. Kim gripped his arm, staring at him and they stood together in the small space by the door. The silent platform was there outside and Hood visualized the men from the castle walking down the train towards them. Then noiselessly the train slid forward and in a moment they had left the lights behind and were rolling down the incline with only the dark valley outside.

Kim let out a 'Whew!' of relief.

'God, we made it.'

They turned into the carriage and dropped on the nearest seats. 'My legs,' Kim said. 'Farthest I ever walked.'

'You were terrific.'

The carriage was empty, and as they put their feet up a waiter came down the aisle. Hood said, 'How's that for service? God, I could do with a drink. How about you, sweetheart?'

'Yes please.'

He turned to the waiter. 'What have you got, whisky?'

'We have some *Ebereschem*. Very good.'

'Boy, that's that stuff from berries, isn't it? Powerful stuff – just right, let's have some *Ebereschem*. And some cigarettes.'

'Certainly, sir.' The man went away.

Hood reached for Kim's hand. He tried to sound casual, though he knew they were terribly vulnerable. 'Wasn't Walter good? There was something strange there, though, wasn't there, those photographs – his wife, I suppose – and that girl. He knew the forest though.'

She said, 'How are you going to pay, darling? And the ticket man will be round before we get down to Aigen.'

'I haven't got a cent. I hope they're going to arrest us.'
She gave him a look. 'I mean it – it'll be our best chance.'

The train slowed on a curve and the cogwheel brake crunched heavily as they took the slope. A few minutes later the track levelled and they ran into another station. Voices came from the rear, Hood lowered the window and looked cautiously out but whoever it was had gone and there was only the station-master lifting his flag. As the train began to move again, Kim tugged at his coat and when he turned she said, 'Sit down with me.'

'What's the matter?'

'It's the reaction, I suppose. I'm scared. I don't like this, I wish it were over.'

'Wait till you've had a drink. Where is that – oh, here it is.' Smiling the waiter approached, put the tray down. There was a tall-necked bottle, glasses, hunks of sausage and cheese and cigarettes. The waiter opened the bottle, lifted the tray forward on to the table. 'I'll leave it with you, sir. You just drink what you want and we'll charge you accordingly.'

'Fine. How many more stations?'

The man lifted his eyes. 'Twenty minutes to Ober-kropfberg, then Kropfberg . . . Zitten . . . Aftenfeld, then we're down.'

'Thank you.'

Hood poured two good shots, handed one to Kim. 'Down in one,' and laughed as she blinked tears from her eyes. 'Whew – you could light the lamp with it. It's worse than grappa.'

Hood swallowed his, felt it sink like a hot ingot. He got up to shut the window opposite and something moving along the carriage caught his eye. He snapped round and froze.

The creature in bandages from the Château des Gerfauts was coming down the aisle. He walked stiffly, holding his bandaged arms at chin height over the backs of the seats, looking monstrous with the dark blubber lips showing at the gap for his mouth, the eyes invisible in the holes above.

Kim was on her feet and screamed. Now the man advanced quickly, Hood swung the glass in his hand and threw it. The glass hit the bandaged face and showered. Without flinching the man came on. Hood grabbed the seat-backs on either side, swung his feet up and slammed into the man's chest. The man took the shock, his arm came down on Hood's shin with a crunch and Hood buckled up, swung away in agony. He thought the bone had gone. The bandages were some sort of plastic covering, hard as armour.

As he staggered, steel finger-tips seized his neck, he lifted himself, wrenched away, smashed the heel of his hand on the man's chin and yelled with the pain. The man's solid forearm chopped downward and Hood only just managed to weave aside, feeling the plastic scrape his head.

They were in the confined space of the aisle and Hood could see Kim heaving vainly on the door at the other end; they were locked in. The clanking of the train through the open window drowned everything.

Hood's foot shot out, tripped the man and he reached wildly for the bottle of *Ebereschem*. The man caught his balance, rearing over him, lifting hands to smash. Gripping the bottle-neck, Hood smashed it over the head with all his strength. The liquid sprayed, the man checked for two seconds, then Hood had the jagged bottle-end in his face and was jabbing it, twisting and turning and seeing the glass chips snapping and grinding off, the bottle powdering against the plastic.

The mighty arms hit his chest and sent him flying back against the window frame. Hood tried to get up but the fingers had his throat, forcing his head back. He heaved. The man was too strong; he groped for the man's throat but it was like gripping a cement pipe. Kim had grabbed the drinks tray and was smashing it on the back of the man's head, making no impression, but he let go one hand and with a savage backward jerk sent her reeling.

Hood strained up, the plastic arm chopped him, he felt himself blacking out. The fingers were squeezing his throat again, forcing his head back. Hood's head was on the edge of the open window. The clanking of the train was deafening. Hood's neck tendons were taut with the effort to keep the man from closing his windpipe, but he didn't think he could make it.

The train moved jerkily. Now Hood's neck was on the window-edge, his head outside. He put out all his strength. The man was trying to hold his head out so that it would hit the rocks; the side of the cutting was inches away and Hood could feel his hair catching. Another inch or two . . .

The white mask of face was over him. He groped madly over the seat for a grip with his hands, touched something and in some last desperate reflex of memory felt what it was – the Corkmaster with which the waiter had opened the bottle. He gripped the cylindrical steel handle, lifted it and jabbed the long hollow needle deep home into the man's eye socket and as the man screamed, pressed the thumb lever. There was a faint hiss of compressed air pumping in, then a bulge of flesh with the eye among it like a bloody egg plopped out of the cavity. Hood sucked his breath in with horror, stabbed for the other eye, jammed the thumb lever again.

The man's head went back, his grip fell away, he staggered, lifting his arms. Gasping, Hood got to his feet. He gave himself five seconds, then locked the man's legs in his arms below the knee, and with a gigantic heave pitched him across the window.

The man's head and shoulders went out, he flailed blindly, then the passing rock wall caught him, snatched him clear of the floor. He hung jammed between the rock and the train for a horrifying moment then with a final upward flip, the train tore him away and he disappeared.

Hood flopped back on the seat and Kim came running from the other end of the carriage.

Forty minutes later as they stood on Aigen platform with three railway inspectors and a pair of policemen round them, Hood saw John Fowler of the Vienna Embassy going by. 'John!' he called out. Fowler checked, turned and came over.

'Christ, this is luck,' Hood said.

Fowler was staring. 'What's happened to you?' He took in the others. 'You look as if you're in trouble.'

'If you please—' the senior policeman growled.

'Just a minute,' Hood said. 'Kim, this is John Fowler, an old friend of mine. Kim McCaine. John, this is providential. I have an absolute priority telegram for the F.O. and we've got to get to London as quick as we can.'

'What? I'm just going on five days' leave.'

'Sorry, old boy, you can forget it.'

THE LAST BANNER

20

WHEN HOOD thought about it afterwards, he realized that none of them could have expected anything like what happened. The whole setting, as they stood waiting in the foyer of Covent Garden was so reassuring, commonplace and secure, it was hard to believe that the descent through the forest and the hideous train journey had been real.

There were the posters saying it was Nureyev and Fonteyn in *Giselle*, the men and women in white ties and long dresses coming in searching their pockets for tickets, the cockney voices of the cab-drivers arriving under the portico. Yet outside was also the reminder – the moon bright and full on the London roofs as it must be now over Schloss Grimmingstein and Johannes Walter's farm and the château in Touraine.

And by glancing round, Hood could see Sir James Lovatt, three police detectives, four secret service men and two sergeants from Bow Street who looked as much like regular Covent Garden ballet-goers as anybody, though they were black belt judokas. Kim was inside, in a seat with two women agents, and police were in other parts of the house.

Ten hours before, with the help of the Embassy in Vienna, Hood and Kim had been provisionally released from police custody and flown to London. Hood had spent the day with the Foreign Office, then Security, and after that there had been a long conference with the Americans and calls to Washington and New York. The Prime Minister and the C.I.G.S. were attending the Covent Garden performance tonight – they had already gone in – but it had been agreed with M.I.5 that there should be no change in the arrangements.

Now the late arrivals were thinning out, the last bell began to ring and Hood caught a glance from Seton the chief security man. *Nobody of Morell's had come.* None of the faces in that elegant crowd had raised even a second's speculation among the watching men and Hood had felt despair and the premonition of failure growing in him. Morell had surely withdrawn, deferred everything while he and his friends covered up. Hood blamed himself; yet what else could he have done?

He turned aside, slipped through the door at his elbow and went quickly to the police sergeant in the back row. The sergeant shook his head; nothing. Hood looked down the aisle and saw Kim in her place, then turned and walked back to the foyer where a flurry of arrivals was disappearing towards the boxes.

Seton stood there impassive, the two sergeants were pacing impatiently, consulting their watches as if they were waiting for late girl-friends. The last few hopefuls were pleading for empty seats at the ticket window.

Suddenly Hood caught the faintest change in the watching men, a movement seemed to be transmitted from outside, a ripple of surprise and the next moment Sir Harry Belgeorge came in. He had a cloak on – Hood thought that was an over-dramatic touch – his Order hanging against his white shirt and for a few seconds, striding into the almost-empty foyer, he looked like a great actor coming forward into the spotlight, or even a great leader of men who had splendid words to speak.

Behind his cover, Hood gasped. Belgeorge had produced a ticket and an attendant was directing him towards the boxes. As he went up the stairs, one of the security men gave up waiting with a shrug and followed him.

Hood groped for a meaning. It seemed impossible that Belgeorge should be in the Morell plot. Was there something else? Was there something in this whole thing he had failed to understand? Could this be a preliminary in Belgeorge's own mad scheme to seize power? It was inconceivable – Belgeorge was far too shrewd and well-informed.

The bell had stopped ringing, the curtain would be going up any moment. Hood glanced round the waiting men and a full minute went by. He was straining to catch the opening sounds of music, stepped back towards the door behind him and caught sight of Morell's face coming in.

Morell was alone, coatless, in tails, looking cold as ice. He walked across the foyer, evidently familiar with the place and Seton had to step forward quickly to intercept him.

'If you'd hurry, sir. Curtain's going up.' He glanced at Morell's ticket. 'Up to the right.'

'I know.' Without pausing, Morell walked unhurriedly up.

Hood saw Seton give a sign to one of the other men not to follow Morell. *They didn't know who Morell had come to meet. If they picked up Morell too soon, they would lose the others.* They waited. The foyer was empty except for two forlorn dames and a young girl watching for some non-arrival by the door. Faintly Hood heard the music start inside. He exchanged a look with Seton. Seton nodded and Hood went through the door. He made his way inside, quietly down the aisle into the vacant end seat beside Kim. Kim glanced at him, Hood took no notice and she turned back. They watched the stage. The whole house was silent and absorbed.

Presently, Hood lifted his head and searched along the row of boxes. Almost at once he saw Morell in the second box to the right from the stage. Morell was sitting back a little from the edge, motionless, his face in half shadow; then, continuing round, Hood saw Belgeorge two-thirds of the way round on the same row. Belgeorge's face, faintly illuminated, was looking fixedly ahead – as if he were staring into the void.

Hood looked back at Morell then caught a movement in the corner of the box. Somebody else was there. Dimly he made out a bare arm – a woman. He tried to distinguish more but couldn't. He looked down and ranged the house with his eyes, seeing the police and Seton's men quietly disposed right and left. Far on the left, a pair of late-comers edged in and there was a little ripple of 'Ssh'-ing. Five minutes went by.

Looking up, Hood saw Belgeorge had seen Morell and was watching him. Belgeorge's face was white, the eye-sockets shadows, the planes of cheek and forehead cut in stone. Suddenly, Hood felt a nudge from the security man behind him. He leant back and the man whispered, 'Four. Just arrived.'

Then, as Hood looked up at Morell's box, a faint oblong of light glowed at the rear. The door of the box had been opened and he saw the figure of a man dimly framed in it, then two more as they entered and finally a fourth; and in those last seconds the light from the corridor outside fell on the woman – Terry Windmiller.

He could see her face, her hair swept back, the gleam of her neck, a necklace and an ear-ring and her eyes turned obliquely as she glanced at the men who had come in. Hood felt a stab. How had he missed her? She must have arrived during his fleeting absence from the lobby to check inside the house.

And realization suddenly flooded into him – Terry had told Belgeorge about Morell's scheme. Hood himself had nearly given the game away to Belgeorge at Schloss Grimmingstein when he had connected Kim with Morell. He remembered Belgeorge's death-white face – the moment when Belgeorge must have realized something was gravely wrong. After their escape, Belgeorge must have grilled Terry. She knew enough and she wanted revenge for T. T. Lucas, poor kid; and Belgeorge had obviously found out more.

Looking up now he could see that Morell had swivelled slightly in his chair and had his face almost completely in the shadow. Hood turned his look along to Belgeorge and at the same instant heard the man behind him get up. Belgeorge had gone. The box was empty.

In seconds, Hood was out of his seat and hurrying back along the aisle. Through the door into the corridor beyond, he nearly collided with Seton and they sprinted wordlessly up the stairs together, hearing the drumming feet of the others behind and above.

On the landing, Hood sprang past two men coming round from the other side of the house and they all raced along the corridor – suddenly hearing the muffled crash of a gun ahead, once . . . again . . . rapidly four times and then as they pounded up and pulled open the door of Morell's box, the mingled cries and screams and banging of seats swept up from the auditorium.

Hood shouldered in, Belgeorge was against the edge of the box, dishevelled, the gun still in his hand, struggling with one of the men. Morell was collapsed on the floor, his face bloodied, eyes staring, a great hole in his forehead. He was obviously dead. Another man was wounded and Terry Windmiller was pressed into the other corner, white as paper.

The lights went up.

With a convulsive thrust, Belgeorge threw the man back and before Hood could grab him, had mounted the edge of the box. He stood balanced there a moment, arms outstretched in a gesture of salvation.

He shouted, 'You are here for the spectacle and you have seen the death of an ideal, the betrayal of a cause – the last great cause – the last great banner to follow! You are all entering the age of death! You will need captains and kings to take you and where will you find them? Society and morality are decaying before you. Death is waiting for civilization – and I, who have nothing now to live for, I precede you!'

A thousand-voiced gasp came out of the hush, Belgeorge thrust the pistol at his heart, pulled the trigger and lurching there a second, toppled over into the void.

As the women screamed, Hood sprang to the edge. Belgeorge lay on his back across the empty seats below from which the occupants had moved. One hand above his head seemed to be lifted prophetically. Behind Hood in the box, Seton's men were removing the others and turning, Hood saw that Terry had gone.

'Where's the girl?'

Seton nodded. 'We've got her. She's on the way.'

*

An hour later the phone rang in the office below where Hood and Kim had waited. Superintendent Young of Bow Street answered and passed it to Hood. It was Seton.

'Everything's in order. We've checked them in. You'd better be at the Yard at nine in the morning, with Miss McCaine of course.'

'Listen, Sam, there's going to be no charge against the Windmiller girl or I'll make a public bloody scandal. It's bad enough knowing she's in some police cell for tonight. If necessary, I'll take it straight to the Home Secretary.'

'You've told me this already.'

'Well, I'm telling you again – and I mean action first thing in the morning.'

'All right. We just heard that the French raided the Château late this afternoon and the Austrians have rounded up fourteen men at that castle. Found about a ton of documents, they say.'

'And the B.B.C. have got hold of some bright Member who's going to ask the Prime Minister in the House tomorrow why the security services weren't on the job at Covent Garden tonight.'

Hood rang off with a chuckle. Kim was stretching at his side and he put his arm round her waist. 'Now let's get a pint of Heidseck, a couple of dozen oysters and care about nothing until the rosy-fingered dawn. Come on, sweetheart.'

Superintendent Young coughed meaningly, 'We ought to go round and get the events down on paper, Mr Hood, if you don't mind.'

'Not tonight, Super,' Hood said. Softly in Kim's ear as he led her out, he said, 'He's the guy who thinks genitalia is an airline.'

* * *